SALT SLOW

salt slow

+

JULIA ARMFIELD

PICADOR

First published 2019 by Picador
an imprint of Pan Macmillan
20 New Wharf Road, London N1 9RR
Associated companies throughout the world
www.panmacmillan.com

ISBN 978-1-5290-1256-9

The following stories have been previously published in journals and magazines:
'The Great Awake' in *The White Review*
'Smack' in *Lighthouse*
'The Collectables' in *The Stockholm Review*, then republished in *Analog Magazine*
'Mantis' in *Neon Magazine*

1 3 5 7 9 8 6 4 2

A CIP catalogue record for this book is available from the British Library.

Typeset in 11/16.75 pt Electra LT Std by Jouve (UK), Milton Keynes
Printed and bound by CPI Group (UK) Ltd, Croydon, CR0 4YY

Visit **www.picador.com** to read more about all our books
and to buy them. You will also find features, author interviews and
news of any author events, and you can sign up for e-newsletters
so that you're always first to hear about our new releases.

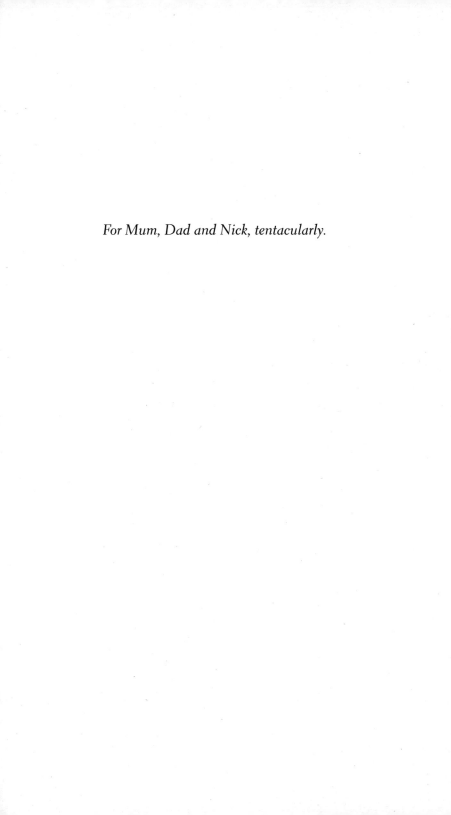

For Mum, Dad and Nick, tentacularly.

it's hard to remember your ribs connect to your backbone

      until the chill in your chest reaches around for your spine

                                 — *Kaveh Akbar*

Contents

Mantis

I have my Grandmother's skin. Problem skin. My Mother buys me witch hazel, calendula, aloe vera, claims she knows a woman who drinks collagen every morning with her tea.

'It's just your genes,' she says. 'Stop picking at it.'

My Mother's skin stretches over the bones of her face like gloss paint poured from a palette. When she dips a finger into the pad of her cheek, I half expect it to come away wet.

Our bathroom shelves are a graveyard of bottles – discarded jars and lotion pumps left to clog at their necks and nozzles, ointments used for two weeks and then abandoned. My Mother buys special sloughing tools, face masks and tinctures from the chemist. Our neighbour, Mrs Weir, is an Avon lady and I suffer one long afternoon of being daubed with honey cream at the kitchen table as she blithely assures me it's supposed to sting.

'It's a funny one, isn't it?' she says to my Mother. 'Not quite eczema but not quite acne either. Psoriasis or vitiligo or something. Sort of like when my Jonathan had that reaction to the *moules* at Il Mare and had to have his stomach pumped. Or – hell – what's that syndrome with the bits that go black—'

'It's hereditary,' my Mother says, assessing her reflection in Mrs Weir's make-up mirror after applying a different colour shadow to each eyelid. 'Difficult puberties.'

'– what am I thinking of?' Mrs Weir burbles on, twisting the cap on a tube of cream like the wringing of a neck. 'The poor people you see in the movies with the skin. You know? The ones with the bells.'

'You're thinking of leprosy,' I say and reach for a pot of shimmer. Mrs Weir snatches it away.

'Not that one, sweets, that's not your colour. You know what I *do* have is a lovely piece of kit that's technically meant for stretch marks, but it might do as cover for you. Look here. The burn victims like this one, see.'

In the event, my Mother buys herself two shades of eyeshadow and spends the evening doing my make-up. I sit still as she mirages me a pair of cheekbones, streaks dark gel across my temples, crimson stain on my lips. Her porcelain concealer comes out velvety on her fingertips and she applies it to my cheeks in slices, rubbing circles through the surface as it blends. My skin peels into the bristles of her make-up brushes and I wind up like Baby Jane beneath the powder. A smoothing of white paste over something sickly, a crusting in the corners of my mouth.

'Mrs Weir's husband isn't allergic to shellfish,' my Mother says later in confiding tones, filling my sparse eyebrows in with softened pencil. 'Allergic to chattering old hags, is more like it. Allergic to bad company.'

She holds the pencil up, triumphant. 'There we go. Red-carpet ready.'

I shift my head to glance into her compact mirror and scatter a confetti of myself across the floor.

+

At Catholic school they teach us to pray, smack the backs of our legs with wooden rulers to stop us sitting on our heels. We wear beige tights and woollen skirts in four shades of house plaid, tie our hair in plaits and speak in indoor voices. In the mornings after matins, we sit together on the sweating radiators, drinking canteen coffee from polystyrene cups and waiting for class to start.

I am known as *The Mummy* because of my surgical gloves and the rings around my eyes and nostrils, but the taunt is a toothless one and predominately affectionate. As Catholic girls, we are all a little awkward, the kind of girls grown slack and strange from too much inactivity and not enough con-tact with boys. My skin, for all its recent ugliness, is just one manifestation of this mutual glitch. We are all of us peculiar; frizzy-haired and sweaty in our woollen blazers, smelling thickly of the things girls come to smell of when they are removed from the company of men.

In the spaces between Mass and classes, we talk long, indulgent circles of self-hatred. It is Girl Language – a cosy bonding rite. We are all convinced we are too fat, too short, too ugly; competing for each title with Olympic fervour, every grievance made to top what came before.

'I can't believe I ate so many potatoes at lunchtime – they should just wire my jaw shut. Just tie my arms to my sides.'

'You're insane, you weigh, like, nothing. It's me who needs the gastric band.'

'Just shut up, both of you, you're both gorgeous. My pores are enormous, like freakishly enormous. My skin is like the surface of the moon.'

'Not as bad as mine. I have so many blackheads I'm amazed no one's carted me off to the plague doctor.'

'You'll laugh, but I hate my toes.'

'Mine are worse. I swear some days I think they're *webbed*.'

'Not as bad as my hair.'

'Or mine.'

'Or mine either.'

We lap up this pummelling talk, its vicious competition – come to love each other for all that we can find to hate. In this way, my skin becomes a kind of bargaining chip, the shreds that sting beneath my sweater a constant point I have to play.

'Well at least you don't all *shed* the way I do.'

It is a winning card, one that can't be trumped. They nod at me, defer to my advantage.

+

I dream in sheddings – spend my nights sunk deep beneath seas of teeth and fingernails, the suffocation of skins cast off and left unbodied. A constant grasping and losing, a catching hold of things that turn to water in my hands. My mattress is wrapped in rubber sheeting, a guard against bed sores and infection, and my sleep takes on something of this slippery quality. In the mornings, my Mother checks me over with a swab of antiseptic, tweezes moultings from my shoulders with a minimal degree of fuss.

'You've been scratching,' she will tell me sometimes, smoothing Royal Jelly over the blades of my back.

'Not on purpose,' I will answer and allow her to bind my hands as usual, this mummification as much a guard against temptation as it is protection for my palms.

+

At school, we watch videos about our changing bodies – censored Health and Safety movies from the 1970s, heavy on abstracted metaphors and light on biology. They play us clips on the overhead projector, jump cuts and fuzzy diagrams, charmless male narrators intoning things like *urge* and *menstruation* and *transitional stage of reproduct-ive growth*.

We are fourteen, some of us fifteen, and we spend our lunchtimes comparing notes on bleedings and kissings and other similar crimes. We eat canteen meatloaf with our mouths whaling open, laugh screeching laughs that end in coughing fits and spat-out hunks of bread. Isolated as we are, we have seen boys, have watched or brushed against them. Stories pass from hand to hand about the friends of brothers and the boys who fix our fathers' cars; invented trysts and sucked-in smells of petrol, deodorant that comes in a silver can.

On Wednesdays, we play hockey on the pitch behind the chapel. Our gym kit is prudish by any standard, but still allows us the sort of assessments that our uniform denies. In the thin white autumn mornings, we judge the fit and fall of Aertex T-shirts, take note of legs shaven above the sock line and scabbed around the knee. Girls we have known since kindergarten are abruptly alien, deeper-voiced and softer-boned beneath the surface, foreign objects with their sudden hips and waists.

I have a standing letter from my Mother and another from my doctor excusing me from games, and so whilst I am still dragged out in the name of Good Clean Air, I am at least spared the spectacle of gym clothes. Standing white-breathed on the sideline, I warm my bandaged hands inside my armpits as, beneath my blazer, I sense a slight but certain splitting in the fabric of my back. I am sometimes given the task of collecting team bibs after matches and I flip them over my head when I do so as an additional guard against the chill.

Afterwards, in the changing rooms, girls pass tampons back and forth like borrowed cigarettes. Smells of hairspray and wet grouting mingle with the tang of day-old blood. Fully dressed, I sit near the door and partake in listless conversation. When the tampons make it to my corner, I simply pass them on.

I do bleed, though there is a difference in the colour and texture, a difference in the pullings and scrapings of my hips. I have thought of asking about this after one of our Health and Safety videos, though these are not usually sessions with much recourse to questioning.

+

My Grandmother was a party girl, according to my Mother. She tells me this whilst brushing my hair, secreting in the pockets of her apron the strands that come away.

'She was a wild one,' she tells me, tapping the back of my spine with the barrel of the brush to make me straighten. 'Some nights she wouldn't come home until three or four o'clock and I'd be there, all of nine years old, waiting.'

She says this without resentment, a simple statement of fact. In the wardrobe mirror, I watch her press a fallen piece of hair against my scalp for a moment, as if hoping it might reattach.

'Where was Granddad when this was happening?' I ask her, already knowing the answer. I have heard this story rattled off before.

'Your Granddad wasn't around by that time,' she tells me, playing along. 'Hold your head up. You're becoming a terrible one for slouching.'

At nights, we read together, though I'm old enough to read alone and my Mother has little patience for literature. I choose Greek myths and ghost stories, tales that come in under fourteen pages and culminate in violent lessons. I read aloud and let her stop me when she wants to – stories of swans and spiders, bay trees, narcissi, girls transformed into monsters by rivals playing dirty.

+

At school, we learn *The Flea* by heart and giggle at the subtext. We learn capital cities and long division and the names of the saints in the order they are cited in exorcism. In Biology, we grow watercress in plastic yogurt pots and keep them on the laboratory windowsills. They turn brown from too much sunlight and we have to throw them out.

Some days, I use my skin to my advantage, skipping Maths to lie down in the nurse's office, complaining of sore arms and pulsing pains. The first time I did this, the nurse insisted on looking, tugging up the back of my jumper without asking and pulling the tail of my shirt from my skirt. What she saw was enough to convince her and henceforth, all my trips to the office were accepted without further enquiry. My friends come to take me to lunch once Maths is over, sniggering behind their hands as I skip from my sickbed, telling the nurse I feel quite better now.

We take Mass on Thursday mornings, sneaking carrot cake from our school bags and making games of dodging the incense cast from the thurible during prayers. The sermons are droning, dragging things, brimstoned with words like *absolution, blasphemy, divine*. After Mass, we play conkers with our rosaries, smashing the beads together in the courtyard until the nuns catch us at it.

+

The teeth are a problem. It becomes harder to talk once I start losing them, which I do in a gradual way on the week of my fifteenth birthday – just a spitting out of molars to begin with, which is at least less obvious to a casual observer than the thinning of my hair. I lay them out in a line on my Mother's kitchen table, the vinyl tablecloth showing images of the Last Supper with a kind of cheerful kitsch. She scrutinises the teeth with forensic detail and then fetches me a glass of water, spooning in a measure of table salt and swilling briskly until it dissolves.

'Gargle,' she says, handing over the glass and sweeping the teeth into the cup of her palm. I do as she says, mulling vaguely on a memory of swallowing my first milk tooth with a mouthful of apple – of asking my Mother whether I might now start growing teeth along the lining of my stomach, like the blooming of a seed.

I spit the water out in the kitchen sink and my Mother fetches almond cream from her handbag, smoothing it absently over my fingers and down the bridge of my nose.

'There now, nothing wrong with you.'

At night, I fall asleep in shreddings and tatterings, my dreams shot through with shouts of violence, bitter notches like bad beads on a rosary. In the still-dark of early morning, I wake to wonder at my face in the wardrobe mirror. Beneath the white flesh of my forehead, my eyes seem further apart than before.

+

Boys arrive with the inevitability of tides. Someone's brother throws a party, someone's cousin makes an introduction, and just like that girls have numbers in their phones and places to sneak off to, skirts rolled at the waist to bring them up above the knee.

In the weeks before Lent, talk turns insistently to boys – to their circling, simplistic conversation and the hundred meanings to be derived from the way they chew their gum. Our mouths gummed with slabs of cupcake, we pledge ourselves to impossible diets in the pursuit of desirability. We repeat the names of boys as we invoke the saints, coiling tongues around the ones we like the best.

'If I lose eight pounds before the party, I think Adam Tait might like me.'

'What about Toby Thorpe – did you hear if Toby Thorpe was going to be there?'

'Seriously though, did it seem to you like Luke Minors was looking at me at the bowling alley last weekend or was it just the mirror behind me?'

'I wasn't looking. I prefer Sam Taylor.'

I listen to these conversations with my fingers in my mouth, nails bitten almost to the knuckle. My gloves are off and my legs are jumpy on the radiator, seeming to fall asleep without warning every ten or fifteen minutes. I am more distracted than usual by things in my periphery: the swarm of dust motes, the carpets creeping up the walls.

'You know I heard Mark Kemper telling Toby Thorpe he thought you were interesting.'

It takes a moment to realise this last is directed at me. I raise one hand, rashed as something burning, raise one eyebrow to match.

'You can pull that face all you like,' I am admonished. 'I'm just repeating what I heard.'

+

There are pictures of my Grandmother on the kitchen dresser. The skin like webbing, the eyes like something stapled in place.

My Mother claims I have my Grandmother's genes, that they come to us all eventually. She says I get more sympathy than she ever did.

'Your Grandmother was a Party Animal,' she tells me, though her usual phrase is *Party Girl*. 'She'd come home at night with glasses she'd stolen from wine bars, beer mats, doughnuts by the boxload. She'd bring back men I didn't like.'

'Where was Granddad when this was happening?' I ask, by rote.

'Your Granddad wasn't around by this point,' she returns as usual, a voice like fingers breaking in a door.

She shows me snapshots from her green velour-bound album. My Grandmother in balding velvet boots, a tinsel wig. A wedding shot with wine glasses, lips red as something chewed to death. Her teeth, so claims my Mother, were porcelain implants, a fact I resent since in recent weeks I have had to settle for a metal brace holding six resin mouldings in my mouth.

'She would have liked you, I'm sure,' my Mother tells me, as if it isn't generally expected that people ought, at the very least, to tolerate their grandchildren.

+

On Ash Wednesday, we walk around school all day with silver smudges on our foreheads. Dipping our fingers in the font by the chapel entrance, we allow the holy water to trickle past our knuckles, either left to dry in track marks or licked absently from palms.

There is a party planned for Saturday, invitations scrawled in glitter on slips of coloured card: *Come to the Anti-Lent Event – Girls Welcome, Boys Encouraged.*

In the bathrooms, girls pluck their eyebrows bare and fantasise the weekend's conquests.

'Hand to God, I haven't eaten since February – Adam Tait won't know what hit him.'

'You're insane. Do you think Toby Thorpe will be there?'

'I don't even know who that is.'

I sit in the corner sink and let my friends test their make-up on me, though the skin beneath my uniform now comes away in pieces and my Mother has taken to wrapping me in coils of bandage to hold the central parts of me in place.

'I'm going to sleep with Luke Minors,' someone screeches, a noise that echoes off the tiles. 'I don't care, I'm going to do it. I swear I am.'

We are frenetic with hunger, with wanting, with the repentance of the season. We laugh like hyenas, our heads thrusting forward from our bodies.

+

Before I leave for the party on the Saturday, my Mother brushes out a wig she has been keeping in a hat box; dark curling nylon with a *flammable* warning label which she snips from the crown. She fixes my face with lipstick and black liner, attaches artful strands of tape beneath the wig to hold my eyes upright.

'There you are,' she says, 'red-carpet ready.'

The party comes about as an infestation – a swarming in the corners of an unfamiliar house. We arrive in cars and carpools, delivered by parents with strict curfews and no idea what to expect. The house belongs to the friend of a brother and is lit all through with paper lanterns, peppered about with ashtrays and crisps in plastic bowls.

I am aware of the feeling of things between my bones, of the blurring and doubling of my vision. I dance with my friends and ignore the tearings and splittings taking place beneath my dress.

Boys spill and surge like the rattling of ice cubes, melting in upon us with every passing song. Adam Tait is sweating through his T-shirt, talking to a girl I know but whose name I can't remember. At the next change in music, he drags her away from the throng and I am left wondering at how it is that I know her and why my fingers seem longer than before.

I think of my Grandmother, who drank her wedding from a wine glass, and drink everything that is offered to me. The music is bright green, bright white, electric. A girl downs a tumbler of wine in one, shrieks *'Unchristian!'* and falls down cackling on the floor.

Boys slope off with girls and I find myself thinking about the itch of the wig I am wearing, the fierceness with which I want to take it off. My tongue is ripe with something thick and liquid, my vision tripling, quadrupling in dim light.

Beside me, a friend is mouthing at me, syllables that mean nothing and make me laugh and twitch my arms in a gesture that seems strangely involuntary.

'What?' I speak too loudly and she shakes her head, gesturing over my shoulder to a boy dancing in the corner.

'Mark Kemper.'

'Who?'

'Mark Kemper. He told Toby Thorpe he thinks you're interesting.'

In the kitchen, girls drink beers from paper cups and argue shrilly. Someone has kissed someone else's boyfriend and a fight is underway. Around the fridge, a thread of girls in matching crucifixes are drinking shots of whiskey, while beneath the breakfast table, a girl is coiled asleep with tinsel in her hair.

I gnaw on the edges of my fingers, wondering when it was that the taste transformed from salt to something tangier.

Someone hands me a beer and I drink it, pressing gratefully against the bodies all around. Beneath my dress, my skin is churning. My legs feel cracked in half, articulated – a spreading and a shifting, as though my bones are springing out of their intended slots.

'*He's there again, look.*' Someone pokes me in the back, a nodded head towards the boy who seems to have followed me into the kitchen.

Before the party, my Mother had shown me photographs of herself at my age – a blinking blade-score of a girl, clear-skinned and strangely boyish.

'I was more like you than you think,' she had said, fanning Polaroids like playing cards on the kitchen table. 'I was a late bloomer too. It's a family trait.'

She had showed me pictures of her wedding day. A blurring of groom, a bride with fingers gnawed to the quick.

I move from the kitchen, passing doors and hallways and finding my way back to the dancing throng. Girls grab at my arms in greeting, cry out and pull me in. I feel my skin sever beneath their hands and wonder whether I should try to clean the pieces of myself from the floor.

We dance in celebration, yell as we do in relief at the end of Mass. A girl pinches playfully at my nose, another pulls on my wig. We bracket and circle and contain each other, twisted together with arms and legs. From a distance, I see the boy edging through the crowd towards me – a blankness of a person, recognisable only by the whispers in my ears.

'*Mark Kemper.*'

'*Look – he's coming over here.*'

'*He told everyone he likes you – I swear to Saint Felix.*'

He grabs for my hand with a force I'm not prepared for, says his name in a voice which drags me away from the group. He says his name again but the music seems to grow louder and I am very aware of my skin. He pulls me back, already dancing, and I have no option but to go with him, a throbbing sense of something rent or ruptured slicing down my spine as the tangle of girls around me loosens and gives way. I let him dance with me, my mouth awash with what feels like saliva, his body like the jolt before a crash.

'I've seen you before,' he is saying in my ear, and I'm not sure how long he has been speaking or whether this is part of a longer sentence. 'You stand out, you know. You're not like other girls.'

I don't know what to say to this as it is incontestably true, yet doesn't feel at all like a compliment. He says his name again. My head swills and I think of my Mother; a darkening, a cracking noise that seems to come from me.

I find he is leading me down a corridor, though I have no idea when it was we left the dancefloor or how it was he

*

convinced me to go. In the corners and shadows and behind doors, I can see girls and boys entwined, strange graspings in half-darkness, woven silhouettes of one on one. Grabby, he has hold of both my hands and I note how small his palms are, though that may just be because my fingers now feel so unnaturally stretched. I am fizzing beneath my dress, my arms and legs consumed with pins and needles, jerking back and forth involuntarily like in the seconds before sleep.

'I knew you wanted it,' he is saying, and I find I have chewed my bottom lip enough to tear it. I grab his hand tighter, taste the blood on my lips.

He tugs me into an empty room – a bathroom with a long mirror – and it occurs to me that he is going to kiss me a second before he does. In the reflection, I witness my reaction, the pale, inverted version of myself in polished glass. There is a coming apart, my head swimming within the collapse, and I understand at once what my Mother meant by 'late blooming' – an adolescence quite unlike the one my classmates have been through.

My skin starts to slip off my bones with a heaviness of sheer relief and the shell beneath is something like my Mother's; the hard, pale surface of unblemishable cold. My teeth drop, my wig slips and I am something else entirely. A suddenness of mandibles and curving neck, eyes sliding into lateral position, long hands that bend straight down as if in inverted prayer. I think, again, about my Grandmother, about my absence of a Grandfather, my Mother's unknown thumb-smudge of groom. I twitch my head towards the boy, feel a shuffling in my back of something quite like wings. I flex my arms and raise myself a little higher as the last of my skin falls down unheeded to the bathroom floor.

It is possible the boy says something, possible he screams. My mouth is wide with anticipation. Not for kissing but for something more in keeping with my genes.

The Great Awake

When I was twenty-seven, my Sleep stepped out of me like a passenger from a train carriage, looked around my room for several seconds, then sat down in the chair beside my bed. This was before they became so usual, the shadow-forms of Sleep in halls and kitchens, before the mass displacement left so many people wakeful at uncertain hours of the night. In those days, it was still surprising to sit up and see the silver lean of Sleep, its casual posture. People rang one another, apologising for the lateness of the hour, asking friends if they too were playing host to uninvited guests.

Sleeps were always tall and slender but beyond that there were few common traits. Experiences varied – a girl I knew complained that her Sleep sat ceaselessly atop her chest of drawers, swinging its heels and humming, while another confided that her Sleep trailed its fingers down her calves, demanding cones of mint ice cream. Couples and cohabiters were the worst off – the Sleeps seemed more prone to behaving badly in numbers, as though they were egging one another on. A rumour persisted in my building that the husband and wife in the penthouse had locked their Sleeps in separate bathrooms to prevent them wrestling violently on the carpet. A man I knew vaguely from the office told me in passing that his and his boyfriend's Sleeps kicked at one another incessantly and flicked pieces of rolled-up paper at the neighbour's Bengal cat. My Sleep had no one to fight with and so mostly preoccupied itself with rooting through my personal belongings, pulling out old photographs and Allen keys and defunct mobile phones, then placing them like treasures at the foot of my bed.

Early on, we didn't know what it was exactly. A lot of people assumed they were seeing ghosts. One night in mid-July, a woman in my building woke the seventh floor with her screaming. Two a.m., dark throat of summer. A bleary stagger of us collected in the corridor and were beckoned into her flat in our pyjama shorts and dressing gowns. We walked from room to room, near-strangers despite our daily proximity, taking furtive note of her decor and her sloppy housekeeping, the cereal bowls on the coffee table, the dirty novel on the bed. We found it in the bedroom, moon-drenched through open curtains. Her Sleep was lanky, crouched beside the bookshelf. It must have been the first time any of us had seen one – its wraithish fingers and ungentle mouth. The girl beside me grabbed my hand when she saw it. She was a girl I knew by sight but had never spoken to – still sticky with sleep around the eyelids and wearing the type of mouthguard prescribed by dentists for bruxism. I squeezed her hand in return and tried to make sense of what I was looking at. The Sleep crossed its palms over its neck as though protecting the feeblest part of itself from harm. This was only a few days before my own Sleep emerged and I felt the uncharitable relief of a narrow escape; a strange affliction which had missed me only slightly, grazed the tender surface of my skin.

By August, the newspapers were labelling it *The Great Awake*, printing graphs and pie charts and columns by confused academics. News pundits speculated broadly, blaming it on phones and social media, twenty-four-hour culture, anxiety disorders in the under-eighteens. Radio hosts blamed it on television. Talking heads on television blamed it on everybody else. Ultimately, there was found to be little concrete evidence to support any one cause – it wasn't more likely to happen if you ate meat or drank coffee or had extra-marital sex. It wasn't a virus or a medical syndrome, it had nothing to do with the drinking water or women being on the pill. It happened in cities, that much we knew, but beyond that there was no obvious pattern. It could happen to one house on a city street and not another. It could affect everyone in an apartment building except for you. It was described more commonly as a phenomenon than as a disaster; one medical journal referred to it as an amputation of sorts, the removal of the sleep-state from the body. People wrote in to magazines to describe their symptoms: the now-persistent wakefulness, the mutation of sleep from a comforting habit to a creature that crouched by the door.

In those early weeks, a live morning show with a viewership of some four million was yanked unceremoniously off air because the host had been attempting to present a segment on seasonal salads with his Sleep in shot behind him. The figure was only a little taller than average and mimed laconically along to the host's actions, shadowing him as he reached for tomatoes while lecturing viewers on proper knife technique. The Sleep mimicked a paring knife, chopping smoothly at the air. It was a Tuesday, people ironing shirts before work. I remember the squeal and stutter before the screen cut to a placard reading *Technical Difficulties – Please Stand By*. I remember the host's eyes, the wakeful crescents beneath the lids. In time, of course, this kneejerk plug-pulling became impractical. By September, half the media personalities in the schedule were turning up to work with wan faces and with their Sleeps in tow. A new series of a property show started with one of the two hosts introducing her Sleep quite candidly, her co-host standing off to the side alone. Television became a gradual sea of doubles, of familiar faces and their silent, unaccustomed companions.

It became so swiftly ordinary – not a thing to be longed for, but nothing whatsoever to be done. Like chicken pox, inevitable. People slept until their Sleeps stepped out of them, then they went on living awake. Shortly after our first encounter on the seventh floor, people in my building stopped sleeping at a rate of about one a night. Mine appeared early, an awkward guest to whom I first thought to offer tea or the newspaper, though I quickly discovered that Sleep was not a companion who wanted much entertaining; it appeared more than content to roam the flat in silence, straightening picture frames where they had fallen askew. I continued to talk to it despite little indication that what I said was appreci-ated, occasionally replying to myself in a different voice to keep the conversation going. I told my Sleep it reminded me of Peter Pan's shadow, and wondered aloud whether I ought to try to attach it to me with a bar of carbolic soap. My Sleep only shook its shoulders and pulled the clock from the kitchen wall to adjust it with a gentle nudge to the minute hand. 'Yes, maybe you should,' I said in a different voice and nodded to show that I had heard. Later, it transpired that no one's Sleeps would speak to them. A strange enough curse, to be wide awake with a companion who pretended you weren't there.

My brother called, quoting our mother – *only think about what moving to the city will do to your health.* His Sleep had appeared only two hours previously and was pacing round the kitchen, rattling chairs and humming the theme to a radio soap for which my brother had once unsuccessfully auditioned.

'Janey, does yours look anything like Granddad?'

I squinted sideways at my Sleep, its steam-coloured skin.

'I don't think so. If anything, it looks like Aunt Lucy, but that's because the only time I saw her was at the open casket.'

My brother chuckled; a muffled sound, hand hovered over the mouthpiece. It was three o'clock in the morning, heavy-lidded sky.

'Pretty spooky,' he said. 'Plus kind of a bore. There's nothing on TV this time of night.'

When we were younger, our mother told us warning stories about the proliferation of ghosts in big cities; ghosts in office chairs and office bathrooms, hot and cold running ghosts on tap. Cupping an ear to the evening stillness of our rural home, she would describe to us towns that seethed with spectres, mime the permanent unsettlement of a city night. Intended as a deterrent to leaving, these stories quickly became the basis of our preferred childhood games. Collecting cardboard boxes and empty Tupperware containers, we would fashion knee-high cities in the basement and chase phantoms around their miniature alleyways, stacking books into the shapes of high-rise apartments and imagining them jittery with ghosts. When the two of us grew up and moved away – to our long thin city of narrow stairs and queasy chimney stacks – our mother cried and demanded we reconsider, insisting that cities could not be lived in but only haunted, that we would simply become two more ghosts in a place where ghosts already abounded. We had gone anyway, of course, my brother to audition fruitlessly for city theatres and me to temp in chilly offices and work shifts in bowling alleys and cafés, almost welcoming the bleakness in exchange for the notion of escape. We had lived apart, to show our mother we could do it, and had fallen into inevitable patterns of silence and strange behaviour. My brother had developed a mortal horror of the silverfish which squirmed between his kitchen tiles. I had grown uncomfortable with the sight of myself in full-length mirrors – the breadth of space around me in the glass.

An interview ran in a Sunday broadsheet: a young woman studying history at university, who described the experience of falling in love with her Sleep.

He's a great listener, a great talker. (I call him 'He' – I don't know if that's politically correct or possible, but that's what he feels like to me.) People say their Sleeps don't talk but I wonder whether that's just because they're expecting speech in the traditional sense. My Sleep doesn't make any noise but that doesn't mean he doesn't talk to me. There are gestures – he moves to the corner of the mattress to give me more space, he alphabetises my books. Sometimes he touches my forehead. Talk can be all kinds of things.

I read this article aloud to my Sleep, asked it whether it was trying to talk to me and I was just too preoccupied by its silence to hear, though of course I received no response.

'I think mine might just be a bit of an arsehole,' my brother said. He was drowsy the way we were all becoming, plum stains in the hollows of his eyes. 'It hides my scripts and scribbles all over my calendar. I've missed three auditions because it's scratched out the dates. It's like living with a shitty poltergeist.'

We were sitting on the front steps of my building, drinking hot chocolate from polystyrene cups. It was 4 a.m. on a Tuesday; thin light, city moving like an agitated creature. We were all still growing used to the night-time, the blue-veined hours of morning that lay only lightly, the white spiders and noctule bats. Without sleeping, it was harder to parcel up your days, to maintain a sense of urgency. The extra hours granted a kind of fearless laziness, a permission to dawdle through the day with the confidence that there would be more time, later, whenever you liked.

'I don't think mine likes me very much,' I said to my brother, finishing my hot chocolate and reaching for the dregs of his. 'It always seems so distracted.'

My brother shrugged, squinting down towards the bottom of the steps where our Sleeps were jostling elbows and kicking at each other's feet.

The girl with the mouthguard knocked on my door one midnight in mid-September and asked me to come and confirm something for her. She was wearing a nightdress – I had torn mine up for dishcloths, having little other use for it – though she had taken the mouthguard out and was holding it gingerly in one hand when I opened the door. Without it, her voice was a curiously clean thing, freshly scrubbed, as though her vocal cords were brand new. Her flat across the corridor was the direct reversal of mine; the kitchen sink and cupboards facing in the opposite direction, the books strewn about in apparent parallel to the ones that littered my bed. It turned out that what she had imagined, on waking, to be the shape of her Sleep in the corner of her bedroom was in fact only the shadow of her dressing gown thrown over a chair. And what she had assumed to be the sound of her Sleep shifting about beside the bookcase was only the rattle of mice in the walls.

She was disappointed, bleary from waking. Everyone in her family already had one, she told me. She went to sleep every night and felt like she was missing out on something, this all-night party she was too exhausted to attend.

'What's stupid is I've always been a very troubled sleeper,' she said, gesturing to her mouthguard. 'You'd think I would have been one of the first.'

Her name was Leonie and when she talked she beat her hands together with a sound like popping corn. She wore the mouthguard to correct excessive tooth-grinding owing to an abnormal bite – an affliction she'd lived with since her late teens when she had lost her back teeth crashing her bicycle into a stationary car. This she told me lightly before blinking and apologising for the overshare, though I only shook my head. I had found that people seemed to speak more freely in the night-time – a strange release of inhibitions that came with talking in the dark. I left a message for our building's maintenance department about the mice in her wall and sat with her until she fell asleep the wrong way up on top of her bedclothes. She was pretty, a fact I noticed in a guilty thieving way. She had fine buttery hair and a gentle cleft in her chin. My Sleep, which had followed me across the corridor and into the flat, oversaw all of this with no particular interest, wandering about and pulling lampshades off their stands.

You don't notice the way a city breathes until it changes its sleeping habits. Looking downwards, you could see it – the restlessness of asphalt. I took to watching from my window for the heave of sundown, the roll and shrug of something searching for a comfortable way to lie. My brother rang, on his way to an audition which had been rescheduled for two in the morning – an early example of what would become the fairly common practice of 'repurposing the night'.

'We're all awake anyway, so why not use the time,' he said, voice blurry from his warm-up exercises. I listened to him run through his audition piece, covering my mouth to stifle a yawn. After he hung up, I leant far out of my window and watched a gang of small girls from the building playing football in the street. Their Sleeps ran alongside them, sticking out unsporting legs and yanking at their ponytails. I listened to their shouts with the night heavy on my eyelids, the whole world hushed and hot beyond my windowsill.

Leonie took to knocking for me at midnight; little Bastille knocks which I answered in the languid way I now did everything, sometimes setting a pot of coffee to brew before I came to the door. Perhaps in a bid to lure her Sleep out into the open, she had put away her old nightclothes and usually came over in soft blue jeans and work shirts. She was a writer, she told me, she wrote an agony column for a newspaper I sometimes read. She had an over-caffeinated rattle about her, a slight panic to her widened eyes that begged me not to ask if she was feeling tired. Now and then, I would catch her staring enviously at my Sleep, unconsciously mimicking its gestures. She was tired of tiredness, she told me. She was tired of feeling left out.

We quickly developed a sort of routine, in the same way that we knew many people in our building had begun to arrange their night-times. A woman who lived on the ground floor had taken to walking her Sleep around the park every night in what we saw as a vain attempt to tire it out. A cellist who lived in the flat directly above me had put together a nightly chamber group along with a viola player who lived on the second floor and the couple from the penthouse, both of whom were apparently amateur violinists. Leonie and I met at midnight, usually in my flat, as she didn't like the way my Sleep would rummage through her books. We did nothing very momentous together – we ate mustard on toast and listened to late-night radio, played solitaire and read our horoscopes and the palms of one another's hands. Sometimes, she brought fragments of her work over and sat on the floor with her back against the sofa, reading me letters the paper had sent her to answer, determinedly suppressing her yawns.

'Listen to this one,' was her usual refrain, affecting the voices of her letter-writers. A teenage girl who was too shy to masturbate with her Sleep watching. A university student whose Sleep stood in front of the door in the mornings and made it impossible to go to class. A man who complained that his wife had a Sleep and he didn't – a situation which he felt undermined his standing in the relationship. This last Leonie read aloud with her tongue pressed downwards, in a voice which dripped contempt but left her face impassive. '*She doesn't say she has a Sleep because she works harder and needs the extra hours awake, but I feel the judgement is implicit.*'

'I wonder if it's unethical,' she said to me once. 'For me to be answering these letters when I don't have a Sleep myself.'

'No more than it is to offer a solution to any problem that isn't yours,' I replied, though she acted as though she hadn't heard me.

No matter how hard she tried, she could never stave off tiredness entirely. Our nights together often ended with her wilting on my sofa, jerking awake at 6 a.m. to insist that she had not been sleeping. I tended not to question this, any more than I did her nightly invasions. I found I liked her company more than that of my Sleep, and vaguely resented the longing looks I would catch her shooting the oblivious figure in the corner of the room. Sometimes when she left to get ready for work, she would kiss me on the cheek or the corner of my mouth, and I would go to get changed with clammy lines along the centres of my palms.

The nights were strange-hued, liver-coloured. A late-September heat pressed downwards – clammy pad of fingers at the ankles – and I spent my small hours drifting around the flat in shorts and T-shirts, listening to Leonie reading letters by people desperate to have sex with their Sleeps, or with each other's. When she was finished choosing which letters to reply to during the day, we would talk or read together. She used words in odd ways – the night nibbling on the windowsill, the pepper taste of her overchewed lip – and I talked to her about things that amused me. I told her that Evelyn Waugh's first wife had also been named Evelyn and that the guy who voiced the Bugs Bunny cartoon had been allergic to carrots. She nodded along to what I said in a way that made me less inclined to bombard my Sleep with conversation in the hours she wasn't there. I had an overbite, had badly needed braces as a teenager, and envied her sparse white mouthful, like little cowrie shells that always seemed a trifle slick. She told me that they were only so small because she had ground them down so much. One reason she was so desperate for a Sleep of her own was that permanent wakefulness would save her from chewing the teeth right out of her mouth. Her voice, I came to realise, was a little like the voice I affected when simulating my Sleep's replies to my questions, and I liked it very much. Most nights, when she could no longer control the weary bobbing of her head and fell asleep on my shoulder, I would let her stay there and then still get away with her sheepish claim, when she awoke, that she had only been resting her eyes.

My brother called to tell me he'd been cast in a play and I met him for drinks to celebrate. We drank red wine which stained our lips the same colour as the spaces beneath our eyes and he shouted his elation to the overcrowded bar. Public places were starting to smell of sleep, of unwashed linens. My brother upset his mostly empty glass in a re-enactment of his audition. His Sleep imitated the gesture, gesticulating none too kindly behind his back until he turned around and caught it.

'And you've been no help at all,' he told it, slurring gently, before turning back to continue his speech with an overdone archness. '*Macbeth doth murder sleep*. Eh?'

Later, I came home to find Leonie waiting for me with an armload of letters and a plate of coconut biscuits. She said she had been itching to tell me a story about a girl she knew who worked for the same newspaper and had attended a series of seminars led by a woman who professed to know the secret to getting rid of a Sleep. Too much tea, the woman had warned was the cause of it, and an overreliance on artificial stimulus. Blue lights. Cut them out. Detox from dairy. The woman had sat in the centre of a circle of chairs, her Sleeplessness on full display as her students' Sleeps wandered around the room. 'Like a game of duck duck goose,' the girl from the newspaper had said. At the end of the fourth seminar, it had transpired that the woman had locked her Sleep in a broom cupboard to support the illusion that she had rid herself of it with only water and vegan cheese. Several members of the group had heard it beating on the walls during a cigarette break and had broken the lock on the door trying to get it out. The girl had admitted to Leonie that she probably wouldn't go back.

'People shouldn't be allowed them if they can't treat them properly,' Leonie said after she had finished telling the story, offering me a coconut biscuit. She looked unconvinced when I told her it was best not to think of them like dogs.

*

I read an article by a woman mourning the loss of her unconsciousness. The article was anonymous, but the tang of
femininity was obvious, the way hips can be. The writer
talked about her sleep before it took a capital: the relief of
absence, the particular texture of the tongue and weight of
the head after a night of sleeping well. *Sleeping gave me time
off from myself – a delicious sort of respite. Without it I grow
overfamiliar, sticky with self-contempt.* The article was published in Leonie's paper and I watched for her envy, the
white of her knuckles as she clutched at the edges of the
newspaper as she read. The writer described her Sleep as
smelling like smoke and honey, recounted its movements
around her house: *The waft, the restless up-and-down. It
throws tennis balls at the walls the way they do in prison-break
movies, kicks at the legs of my chairs.* Leonie asked me what
my Sleep smelled like and I told her: orange peel and photo
paper. Odd, talismanic scents – my mother loading me down
with tangerines for my journey to the city, sending me photographs of our old house in the post. A little later, having left
the room to put on the kettle, I came back to find Leonie
standing by my Sleep as it rooted through the boxes I kept
under the bookcase to store old diaries and ticket stubs. Not
noticing me, she moved in as close as she could, tilting her
head towards my Sleep and breathing in. I watched this
happen for several seconds, watched the way my Sleep
quirked its head in irritation but failed to pull away. Still
breathing in, she rested her forehead against its neck for a

fraction of a second and I imagined the sensation, cold glass wet with condensation against her skin.

The morning trains were overloaded with bodies both solid and spectral. I became used to standing whilst my Sleep muscled its way to a seat, grew accustomed to the rows of Sleeps with their legs crossed, the people clustered round the doors, grey-faced and leaning heavily. I spent lunchtimes wandering the city, watching people shuffle from coffee shops to bodegas – the greasy slink of cooked meat, egg sandwiches. I sat on steps and municipal benches, eating the orange cake my mother sent from home in tinfoil packages, talking to my brother on the phone. All around me people shimmered with exhaustion. One afternoon, I skipped lunch entirely to wander through one of the city cathedrals, listening for the hush of choir rehearsals, the muffle of choristers pushing their Sleeps' muting hands from their mouths. I pictured my mother cupping her ear around the stillness of the country, evangelising tirelessly about haunted city sounds, the never-ending movement. The cathedral flickered. Thrum of bodies and almost-bodies.

Leonie read me a letter, leaning up against my fridge one night with her reading glasses on. She had taken to wearing them more often in recent weeks, whether or not she happened to be reading. It prevented her eyes getting tired so quickly, she said, in a rare moment of admission that tiredness was something she felt. It was difficult for her, this unnatural wakefulness. During the day, she would look up from her writing desk and swear she saw the city moving past the window, as though either it or she were running very fast in one direction.

'Our relationship is struggling,' read the letter, 'because of my husband's Sleep. Sometimes his expression when I wake in the night scares me. He says some nights he leans over me and tries to will my Sleep out of me so that we can both be awake together. I sometimes feel I must be the only person in the city left asleep, though I still feel tired all the time, which in itself he considers a kind of betrayal.'

Leonie came to sit beside me and laid her head down on my shoulder for a long time. It was hard, she said, to be sympathetic to all the people who wrote to her complaining of problems with their Sleeps, whilst at the same time feeling so bitterly conscious that there were still people like her left sleeping through the nights in this restless city. It made her worry that there was no countdown to zero, that some people might simply be destined to never have a Sleep at all. I told her that I didn't know what she thought she was hoping for, that I considered my Sleep an unfriendly interloper at best. That sometimes I lay down on my bed and imagined unconsciousness, lay on one arm and then another until they lost all feeling and I could at least enjoy the sensation of sleep in some small part of my body. That the only thing I really liked about my new situation was her company – that and the occasional thought of the city holding me up despite how washed-out I felt, like hands beneath my arms and around my middle, keeping me off the floor. Of course, by the time I said all of this she was already asleep on my shoulder, snoring softly into my neck. Above us, the string quartet played a Dvorak nocturne, a slow movement in B.

My mother called to check I was eating properly and to say she'd told me something like this would happen. She didn't have a Sleep, of course. Very few people outside the city limits did. My mother's voice on the phone was well rested, excessively virtuous. She told me she knew a man who lived not a stone's throw away from her who had gone into the city one day on business and returned with a Sleep which didn't belong to him. I asked her what had happened to the person whose Sleep had been stolen and my mother told me not to ask stupid questions. 'What do I know about the horrible things? I should imagine they're glad to be shot of it.' She mentioned my brother, complaining that he never answered her calls. She asked me what I was doing with myself, whether I was seeing anyone, and I thought of telling her about Leonie, but my Sleep chose that moment to take the receiver away from me and hang up the call.

I invited Leonie to my brother's play and she accepted, resting her hand on my thigh for a moment and digging in her nails the way a cat might. She was sleepy in the down-curve of her mouth, her slack expression, and when she shifted towards me she smelled of hard city water. We were eating oranges on the sofa and she kept offering me pieces, though I had my own aproned out in my lap. The performance had been scheduled for two in the morning to capitalise on the list-less night-time crowds. Leonie gamely brought along a flask of coffee and we sat in the dark together in the little raked space above a pub, sharing a box of chocolate-covered raisins and nudging each other every time my brother came on. On the stage, the actors' Sleeps performed what looked like their own play in the spaces behind them. Without dialogue, their storyline was hard to follow but it kept drawing my eye – the translucent figures shifting about around the actors, miming along to words I couldn't hear. It was nearly five by the time we got home and Leonie had finished her flask of coffee, eyes melting down her face. I asked her if she wanted to come in but she told me she needed her mouthguard, looking away in embarrassment and flashing her fingers by way of fare-well. Less than an hour later, she knocked on my door again, complaining of nightmares. It was relentless, she told me, like everyone else's unused dreams now came to bother her, bringing nightmares of fast-climbing vines and empty trains and disturbed places in the earth. I let her sleep on my sofa with her head pillowed in my lap until seven, when I had to start dressing for work. Moving between rooms with my toothbrush in one hand, I glimpsed her sitting up on the sofa, peeling another orange and offering slices to my Sleep.

*

I went for dinner with my brother – though people now tended to eat whatever they wanted at different times of the day and night. He ordered eggs and milk, I ordered a cheeseburger, and we sat at a sugar-stuck table, still cluttered with the last patron's coffee cups, a napkin smeared with orange lipstick, a plastic straw tangled up into a bow. Through the window overlooking the parking lot, the sky seemed of a strangely darker cast to the one I was used to, an unfamiliar absolute of night that I connected with being away from the city, from the swirling blues and changeabilities of light pollution. My brother showed me a newspaper review of his play. After reading it I flipped the paper over and read aloud from Leonie's column, which contained advice for dealing with Sleeps who were rude to your grandmothers, who ate your food or ignored you or always seemed to want to fight. My brother listened to me idly, jostle-elbowed with his Sleep on the opposite side of the booth. He looked, I thought, strangely of a piece with the figure beside him. Reflected in the window, it was hard to tell which of them was paler, which would be more recognisable if I came up to the diner from the parking lot and saw them through the glass. I was still looking towards the window when my own Sleep, which had been wandering restlessly between tables, came to sit down beside me. I didn't turn my head towards it, noticing the way it had started to smell like hard city water, like the rusted place around the plughole from which I occasionally had to wrench clogs of hair with a coat hanger bent at the neck.

*

Leonie asked me to proofread something she was writing. I had a better eye for detail, she said, I was used to reading in the dark. The piece wasn't for her advice column but one she had been asked to write for a magazine – a piece on living without a Sleep, she told me with a grimace. She'd write it anonymously, she said. It wasn't something she wanted to own. Towards the end of the piece, she described it as like the sensation of looking for your shadow on the ground in front of you only to realise that it was midday.

'It's a good piece,' I said, when I'd read it. 'But you're writing like you're making it up. Like it's fiction and you're trying to imagine how someone like you must feel.'

'Wishful thinking,' she replied, as my Sleep entered the room from the kitchen, rattling its fingertips across the top of the radiator.

She shrugged a shoulder and raised her head to look at me, leaning forward after a moment to kiss me on the side of my mouth, nodding her thanks. I dipped my chin, tilting slightly to catch her properly on the mouth and she kissed me gently for a moment before pulling away. She smiled at me vaguely, shrugged her other shoulder.

My brother called to tell me to turn on channel four. He was watching a news piece on people who were doing drastic things to rid themselves of Sleeps. They interviewed a woman who had been arrested for luring her Sleep to the top of her apartment building and pushing it off. The way it fell, she said, you would have thought it didn't know about gravity. The legs continuing to walk through nothing, the windmill before the sudden dragging drop. This woman was the only one who had agreed to be interviewed without insisting her face be pixelated. She had been released from police custody, there being no workable law in place to condemn her, but was largely housebound due to the protesters surrounding her property and forcing hate mail through the letterbox.

'When I retell it,' she said, 'I have to remind myself that what I did wasn't unnatural. No more than taking a pill to fall asleep is unnatural – sometimes we just need that little push.'

The noise from her front lawn could be heard inside the house, the chants picked up on the reporter's microphone – protesters singing about the injustice done to a defenceless Sleep. Even so, she seemed singularly unbothered. As the interview drew to a close, she tilted her head towards the window and the sunlight hit her in a way which illuminated her face, the spaces beneath her eyes fresh as rising dough, gloriously well rested.

'Makes you think, doesn't it?' my brother said, once the news had moved on to another story. 'Not a nice thought, but makes you think.'

'I didn't know you could kill them,' I replied. No one had known until now, it seemed, because no one had really tried. 'It doesn't seem right though, does it?'

*

Leonie's piece was published anonymously and she brought the magazine around at midnight on the day it came out. The story was sandwiched between several others; the man who had stolen another man's Sleep, the woman who had packed her Sleep into the back of a car, driven it out to the country and left it there. Leonie's piece, I thought, sat oddly amongst these stories of frayed nerves and hard exhaustion. In the midst of all these haunted people, she sat alone, without a ghost yet longing for one, her writing like a clasp of fingers around empty air. I reread the piece while she made me tea, the gentle clatter of her in the other room a pleasant presence, just as the restlessness of the night had become a comforting familiarity. City noise, the wriggle of wakeful shoulders, Leonie breaking a cup and cursing to herself next door.

When she came back, she was white, red-lipped from biting at herself. My Sleep came after her, holding the pieces of the mug she had broken, which it ferried to the coffee table and placed there before moving to the corner of the room. Leonie passed me a cup of tea and came to sit beside me, eyeing the magazine in my hands.

'I hate it,' she said, 'I wish I hadn't written it.' Her voice curled up around its edges the way paper does when you set it alight at the sides. I looked at her dumbly for a moment, sipped my tea on a reflex and immediately burned my tongue.

'But it's good writing,' I said after a long pause, wondering from her face whether she might be about to cry. 'What do you hate about it?'

'I hate that I had to write it,' she replied, harshly. 'I hate how tired it makes me to read.'

In the corner, my Sleep twitched its head to the side. An odd motion, as though trying to get water out of its ears. I looked at Leonie and thought about the weight at her shoulders, picturing the sensation of sleeping, the fall and clean absence of thought. After we'd finished our tea, I asked her to lie down on the sofa with me. She looked at me strangely but didn't object. We positioned ourselves as comfortably as possible, Leonie slipping up into the crook of my arms. I pictured sleep – the old stillness and the blacks of my own closed eyes. In the corner, my Sleep shifted itself, turning its head into its own shoulder, then the crook of its elbow, as if to inhale a smell.

'I should have my mouthguard,' Leonie murmured vaguely, though I only shushed her, saying after a moment that I'd wake her if she started spitting teeth.

I held her for a long time and, after the night had passed, woke up to find that I had truly slept. The corner of my room was empty, as was the space before me on the sofa. Leonie had gone, leaving behind the magazine but taking with her my Sleep. For a long time, I chose not to sit up, remaining instead where I was at full length on the sofa, registering as if in pieces the solidity of my body. A little later, I would rise and go about my business, noting when I did the old sensation of refreshment, a certain lifting from the tops of my shoulders and from the spaces beneath my eyes. It was morning, the air refreshed and gentle as if from dreamless sleep.

The Collectables

We burned what we could of Simon Phillips in a pit at the end of the garden. Jenny held her hands over the flames – a bonfire of the final boyfriend: photographs with eyes scratched out, a note he had written on a napkin, the grisly confetti of toenail clippings she had pulled from the bathroom bin. The pads of her fingers were mottled yellow, barbecue-black under the nails. Miriam dragged her away at last and smoothed her palms with aloe vera, talking a circle of taut affirmations – *you'll feel better – he wishes – doesn't know what it is he's lost.*

This was the last of them, the final dramatic gesture. Miriam and I had lost our boyfriends already and contributed to the seeing-off of Jenny's with a corresponding vigour. When the neighbours called to complain about the smell, Miriam told them with great dignity that we were purging ourselves of evil spirits.

'*Well I'm sorry that you've had to close your windows, Mrs Adams, but that's the price one pays for catharsis.*' She held the phone slightly away from herself, as ever unwilling to touch the earpiece for fear of infection. Someone had once told Miriam that she looked like Princess Anne and this throwaway comment had come, over time, to form the basis of her whole personality. She wore green velvet loafers year-round, pinned her hair in the shape of a pumpkin, spoke like her molars were made of glass. After hanging up, she sat for a moment in silence, twisting each of her rings halfway round her fingers so the gemstones faced inwards. Catching me looking, she shrugged and held her hands out – two palmfuls of diamonds, as though she had clawed them out of the earth.

In the drifting dusk, we picked through the debris of the fire with cereal spoons; burned husks of photo paper, the plastic-coated lace of a tennis shoe which had failed to catch alight. The failing sunlight illuminated twists of ash and charred pieces of the newspaper we had used as kindling. I pulled a shred out with my fingers and read aloud the two lines of text which had not been scorched beyond comprehension. It was from the page which ran the personals ads, a drab little reverie of a sentence, ending in a smear where the phone number should have been.

'*Professional Woman, mid-forties, seeks Prince Charming for Fairytale Endings/Heroic Rescues/Castles in the Air. Please call Linda on—*'

'Keep dreaming, Linda,' Jenny snorted, kicking a heel over the ashpit of her ex-boyfriend, who by now would be in St Austell with the girl he had dumped her for.

+

'There is a level of insult I cannot overlook,' Miriam announced, 'in the way that men behave towards women.'

We were sitting on the front steps of the house, drinking Cherry Cokes in the hot September twilight. The cigarette which we were passing back and forth had started with Jenny, but was now smudged with three separate shades of lipstick – red for Miriam, tangerine for Jenny, frosted brown for me. Across the street, Mr Cline from number eleven was hacking at the bushes his wife had carefully cultivated, a dense and elaborate display of power topiary which, thanks to his ministrations, was now vandalised beyond repair. Two doors down, a muster of pre-teen boys were playing Chinese chequers on the pavement, the young mum from number seven dragging her pram precariously down into the road in order to pass them by.

'I mean look at that.' Miriam gestured with index and ring fingers clenched together 'Don't even move to let her pass. *Men.*'

'Those aren't men,' I replied, squinting towards the boys and noting their acne-dusted shoulders, the way one of them had sprouted far taller than the others and had to bend almost in half to play their game.

'True,' said Miriam, equably, 'but if you stuck them all together they'd probably add up to one.'

This was some days after the bonfire. In the dead end of that week, Jenny had taken to poltergeisting round the house in her bedsocks, cluttering surfaces with cups of cold tea and crumby saucers, snivelling and watching the phone. Simon had finally called on Wednesday night, sloppy on sangria and wanting to know why Jenny had sent him a shoebox of ashes in the post. Miriam had been the one to answer and throughout the brief conversation had stood with one hand extended, forcibly holding Jenny away from the phone. On hanging up, she had wiped her ear distractedly with her monogrammed handkerchief, complaining that she could practically feel him spitting through the receiver.

'I don't want to hear it,' she had said, when Jenny had made signs of starting to snivel again, before ordering me away to the corner shop to buy Cokes and a box of peanut brittle with the money from the swear jar in the hall.

+

Until recently, I had been seeing a man called Stephen Connolly, who had been a good kisser and appalling in all other aspects. The realisation had come upon me only in stages, for I liked kissing well enough to ignore for a while the books he read and the way he spoke about women, the fact that his chin was feeble and his back pocked from waxing hair away. The reality of the situation became clear eventually, but even then, it was somehow him who left me. I was tricky, he said, I asked too much of him, the things I talked about sometimes drove him mad.

That's the problem with kissing. In theory, when someone's good at it, you should be able to keep kissing forever. But of course, forever is too long to do anything without getting bored.

+

We were a household of incomplete ideas, of brisk, abortive grasping. We had fallen together by way of a house share; a hierarchy grown from the blank of our random assignation. Miriam, tautly matriarchal, cooked key meals, labelled shelves for private use and studied Gainsborough with biros stored behind her ears. Jenny, wan and fanciful, hacking her way through a thesis on Urban Gothic in the Fin de Siècle, occupied the box room and papered its walls with collaged images of insects and garden pests. I existed somewhere between, storing reference books on the landing, pursuing studies in social realist literature, eating endless toast. We spent our days working on our Ph.D.s, our nights watching films on the floor of the living room, bare-legged and digging splinters from our feet with tweezers, drinking iced tea from a melamine jug. We talked about men unkindly and too often, our aggravation with the topic at large belied by the frequency with which we returned to it. The nights around that time were balmy through slices of open window, clouded with the smell of charcoal barbecues before the meat goes on to cook. We would argue in desultory fashion over which movie to watch, knowing as always that we would end up watching Jenny's choices, if only for a quiet life.

On Fridays, Miriam would order us pizzas, businesslike with the hated telephone in hand as we yelled the same jokes we yelled every week.

'I'm ordering now – what does everyone want?'

'Cheese and Tomato, please. Or Margherita if they have it.'

'Cheese and Tomato *is* Margherita. What about you?'

'I don't know. What are you having?'

'Ham and Pineapple.'

'That's no help.'

'Well, what toppings do you feel like?'

'The flesh of righteous men.'

'I'll get you a Meat Feast.'

It was always the same man who delivered our pizzas – in his twenties, green-eyed as a cat at night. Since the first visit, he had appeared singularly unfazed by the way we answered the door all together, handing over our food with a smile and a mimed tug of an imaginary cap.

'You ladies have a wild night,' he would say and saunter away before we could tip him.

Back in the living room, Jenny would simper over his green eyes and Miriam over his manners until the pizzas grew cold and had to be microwaved. We had been in this town for what felt like for ever, and in all that time, only the man who delivered our pizza had managed to never once let us down.

+

Three magpies on a washing line – a good or bad augury, depending on the rhyme you chose. Drinking coffee in the garden that Thursday, I listened to the funeral bells from the church three streets away. It was early still, a sore-boned morning, gentle dew-fall after rain. My throat ached from arguing down the phone with Stephen over the jacket he claimed I had stolen as an act of retaliation after we split. My ears still rang with the memory of his voice, its dogged enervation.

'It's for the guy from the admissions office at the university.' Miriam in white cotton shorts, coming to sit beside me and tilting her head to indicate the bells. 'The one with the cowlick. He stepped in front of a bus on Monday.' She shrugged and took a sip of my coffee. 'So they tell me. It's a shame.'

We sat together until the funeral bells faded, preparatory to a second burst of rain. Back inside, we found Jenny making pancakes the way Simon had liked them – brown with almond butter on the insides and slightly burnt at the rim. Miriam took the skillet from her wordlessly and tipped the pancakes into the sink, her white shorts stained black and gritty from the garden steps.

We drank through the day, bottles of yellow wine which made us hectic and shrill, our neighbours hammering on the walls to protest against our too-loud music. By the evening, we were headachey and red about the eyelids, Jenny wailing that she hadn't done a stitch of work all day.

'Well for God's sake,' sighed Miriam, prickling with alcohol, 'we were only drinking to keep you company.'

I was the one to suggest the walk, if only to prevent an argument. We wandered down through the town, barefoot and weaving, curtains twitching around us in the close-walled streets. We ended up at the church, its bells now silent, peering down into the cemetery to spot the fresh-dug afternoon grave.

'What a waste,' Jenny murmured when we told her about the admissions guy, scrolling through her phone to find a photograph she had once taken at a faculty party – a crop of the bottom half of his head. 'He had such lovely teeth.'

+

Jenny loved the classic Universal horror films – *Dracula* with Bela Lugosi, *The Invisible Man*, *The Creature from the Black Lagoon*. Coming back from the church that night, she put on *Frankenstein* with Boris Karloff, rewinding twice through the opening scene with its grim graveyard, its coffin dredged up from the mud.

We were all, by this point, halfway into the next day's hangover, furred to the back teeth with instant coffee, flat out like dogs on the floor.

'Think of the man we could have if we only took the best bits,' I remember Jenny saying at some point, nodding at the monstrous man being woven together onscreen. 'Stephen's kiss, Simon's torso, Matthew's—' She stopped and looked at Miriam enquiringly, though Miriam only snorted softly and told Jenny not to talk over the film.

Matthew was a lecturer at the university who had given Miriam a diamond ring the previous winter and then asked for it back in June. This had been around the point that all three of us had started falling behind on our theses, although why it affected Jenny and me as much as it did Miriam would be difficult to say.

+

We had a small cellar in our house which had been used as a makeshift shelter during the Second World War. It was here that Jenny first drew the outline on dressmaker's paper – the long body of a man in black marker which she laid out on the floor like the scene of a crime. She had been drinking fairly solidly all week; a thin dribble of spirits which started with Irish coffee in the mornings and continued through to makeshift cocktails the moment the clock struck six. Simon called fairly frequently now, though when he did Miriam only told him to get on with things with his new girl-friend and for God's sake stop bothering us. I made slow progress on my thesis during this time, traipsing to the library and back in my open-toed sandals, stewing in the gardens in the late afternoons. I was there the day Jenny came out in pyjamas and wandered down to the ashpit at the end of the lawn. For a moment, I watched her scratch chicken-like through the remnants of our bonfire, before suddenly she bent and then straightened, pulling something out of the dirt.

On her way back up the lawn, she held her palms out to me, the way Miriam had showcased her handfuls of dia-monds. Only in this case, the cupped palms held not precious stones but a charred collection of fingernails – the chalky half-moon cuttings Jenny had wrenched from the bin to set fire to after Simon first walked out.

+

The scavenge became Jenny's little joke – coming home with strands of hair yanked from men at the supermarket, fallen eyelashes she had found in the creases of library books and collected on pieces of folded tape. In the afternoons, when Miriam and I were submerged in our reference books, Jenny would haul her plunder down to the cellar and arrange lines of nails and fringes of hair around her line-drawn paper doll, tacking them down with Pritt Stick and Elmer's washable glue.

'Occupational therapy,' she said one afternoon when I asked her what she thought she was doing with a pocketful of skin-peppered dust from a university windowsill. 'Something to do every day, one day at a time. Kind of like being in AA.'

'Not that you would know,' Miriam replied, gesturing to the beer bottle in Jenny's free hand.

The sun sharded through the open window, amber in the thunder-smelling midday and filling Jenny's face with momentary electricity, as though she had been set alight at the neck.

For the most part, we left her to it, poring over our books with increasing distraction as the temperature rose and the telephone rang more and more often. Simon had a bee in his bonnet about something – insisted on talking to Jenny, though every time he rang Miriam answered and never allowed him enough time to explain.

'Maybe if we just let him speak to her,' I ventured to Miriam one morning, the two of us on the back steps, drinking tea in our dressing gowns. 'You let me speak to Stephen after I stole his jacket. And even Matthew stopped calling to ask for his ring back once you had a word with him yourself.'

'It's not the same,' Miriam replied, curd-yellow at the eyelids, 'You'd never mistake Stephen's voice for a homing call.' Back inside, we found Jenny just coming in, though it was nearly eight o'clock. She smiled at us both, pulling her hand from the front pocket of her dungarees to show us what looked very much like the flicked-off head of a scab.

+

We ordered pizzas as usual on the Friday. The delivery man brought them to our door well under the forty-minute-guarantee time, smiling at each of us in turn as if sharing something pleasurably private. His eyes were as green as ever – the colour of wine bottles emptied down sinks.

'You ladies have a wild night,' he said, like he always did, and Jenny wriggled with delight.

The phone started ringing shortly afterwards, but for once even Miriam ignored it. We watched movies until well past midnight and I must have drifted off because the next thing I knew it was dark and Jenny had apparently gone out and come back again. I didn't ask her where she'd been or even move to let her know I was awake, but even so, there she was creeping in with mud-crusted elbows and a bottom-jawful of straight white teeth in one hand.

The scavenge became less of a game after that – Jenny coming home at odd hours smelling like dirt and cold stone, black tote bags which took on curious shapes when thrown over her shoulder. I encountered Mr Cline in the street one Thursday morning, complaining loudly that his hedge clippers and spade had gone missing. Two days later, I came across both in the hall cupboard, curiously pristine as though recently washed. I told Miriam it might be best if we avoided the subject of dating for a while, though as Miriam pointed out, almost any topic of conversation was enough to set Jenny off on the subject of The Perfect Man, these days.

Simon had begun to call daily, so most of the time now Miriam just let the phone ring. He was sorry, she told me in confidence, his new girlfriend wasn't what he'd hoped, he wanted Jenny back. That day, it had been announced in the local paper that a young athlete, an Olympic sprinting hopeful born barely six streets away, had died of an untimely heart attack and would shortly be brought back home to be buried. Jenny had spent the morning in a reverie about men with good legs, mentioning several times how disappointing Simon's had been the few times he had agreed to do it with his trousers all the way off.

+

'I think we've taken our eyes off the ball a little,' Miriam said to me seriously. The collection of fingers on the kitchen table came not from one hand but several, though all seemed to be at similarly early stages of decay. She had gone into

Jenny's bag and found them, counting them out for me like paper money, and now stood uneasily as a sound reached us – Jenny's footsteps on the cellar stairs.

'There they are,' Jenny said, coming into the kitchen as calmly as though seeking her house keys. 'I knew I didn't just have thumbs.'

She collected them together, a bouquet of severed fingers, tall and blue-tinted towards the tips. A rogue image swam through me – Jenny coming back from her first date with Simon, the slender handful of daffodils he had given her and the way she had held them upright all the way home. As if on cue, the phone started ringing and Jenny glanced towards it impatiently. 'I don't know why he bothers. Now *these*,' she held three fingers towards us as though inviting us to pick a card, 'are from a concert pianist. They buried him last week. Incredibly limber-looking, don't you think? Whereas *these*,' three more, squarer around the nail and knuckle, 'well these I just chanced upon. I like to imagine this guy was good with his hands, whoever he was. What a collection, anyway. Don't you think?'

'Jenny, you're going to fall behind on your thesis.' It was all I could think to say, although later that day, when she showed us what she had been doing in the cellar – the scavenged skin and bones and severed features all arranged just-so on her strip of card – I understood that she hadn't so much fallen behind as changed subjects altogether.

+

It was a Saturday when she finally spoke to him, just back from a funeral and holding her tote bag protectively along the bottom as though concerned it might split. She sat down on the arm of the sofa, receiver in hand, legs crossed and expression absent. From the kitchen door, Miriam and I could hear the bleed of Simon's voice from the receiver, the way he rattled on in increasingly desperate fashion as Jenny answered him only in yeses and nos.

'It's no good,' she said finally, waving her hand in Miriam's direction and signing a request for a cup of tea. 'There's nothing else I really want from you, nothing you can say. You've just given me the time to realise I can do better than you. That I can call the shots myself.'

She nodded along with the voice on the phone for a moment, readjusting her bag on her shoulder slightly as she did so, a shape curiously resembling an ear faintly visible through its canvas side.

'Look,' she said at length, 'you were wonderful on paper. You're just not the sum of your parts.'

+

Jenny ordered pizza alone while Miriam and I were at the library, one Friday afternoon in summer rain. The delivery man came to the door as normal – green eyes like church windows – tipping his imaginary cap to her and asking how come we'd only ordered one pizza this time.

She gave no clear answer, only smiling benignly and asking whether he didn't want to step in out of the rain. There would be lightning, she said, not good weather to be out in. Why not bring the pizza through, she said, I've got something to show you, something that'll make your pretty green eyes pop right out of your head.

Formerly Feral

When the woman who lived across the street from us adopted a wolf and brought it to live with her, people were not as surprised as you might imagine. People had been doing stranger things in our neighbourhood for years. My Father, the novelist, took great pleasure in telling stories about the neighbours – how Ms Brenninkmeijer lived with a man fifty years her junior who had only knocked on her door in the first place to deliver a parcel, how Mr Wintergarten was widely suspected of poisoning local dogs and leaving them, taxidermied, on doorsteps for their owners to find. My Father said a town was only as interesting as its bad apples and only as safe as its lunatics. When my sister and I were younger, he would point to all the houses on our street, counting on his fingers and explaining that by the law of averages, at least two of our neighbours were likely to commit murder. *Have perhaps already done so*, he would add, when our reactions were not satisfactorily extreme. In the divorce, my Mother cited the impossibility of living with a man whose approach to life was so ineradicably ghoulish. In return, my Father cited my Mother's treatment of life as though it were someone unpleasant she was stuck sitting next to on the bus.

When our parents divorced, my sister went to live with my Mother – a hard cleaving that I, aged twelve, felt far more acutely than the divorce itself. In the months directly following her departure, my sister sent me letters on my Mother's headed paper, brand new and with the maiden name loudly reinstated – *From the desk of Allison Weyland – Allison Stromare no more!* My sister wrote in postcard couplets (*Sun is shining – wish you were here*), offering negligible detail beyond the doodles of herself she always included; little thumb-smudged cartoon sisters generally engaged in some strenuous activity – putting together a bookcase, walking a dog, performing jumping jacks. I kept these letters bulldog-clipped together in the space between my bed and the wall and reorganised them frequently, trying to create a coherent flipbook out of all the little figures in the corners of pages, throwing balls in the air and hula-hooping and dancing and building model trains.

My Father's house was a strange place once partially deserted; yawn of space, hand held insufficiently over the mouth. My Father took to writing in the kitchen where before he had retreated to his study, started leaving his shoes wherever he removed them and cooking heavy dishes which disregarded my allergies. I developed a habit of eating on my own to avoid his bloody meats and creole jambalayas. I smuggled sleeves of water crackers to my room and ate them smeared with peanut butter, stole dates and bits of cake from the untended larder and siphoned inches of cognac into mugs which I stacked on the floor and allowed to grow rancid with fruit flies. Occasionally, my Father would ask me how school was going, how I intended to spend the weekend, but for the most part we coexisted in a kind of conciliatory silence. Without my Mother, I became negligent with washing, wore my shirts untucked. I experimented with the make-up she had left behind in bottom drawers of her dressing-table – daubed my eyelids the colour of tangerines.

About six weeks after the divorce was finalised, the woman who lived across the street came around to express her condolences, bringing on one arm a fruit basket, which would later turn out to contain only pomegranates, and on the other arm the wolf. My Father invited them in for coffee and ten months later, he and the woman from across the road were married. She and the wolf came to live with us, putting her house up for sale.

+

Advice on keeping wolves as pets can be found in publications put forth by various animal-rights organisations – the tone is seldom wholly encouraging. In *The Ethical Pet Owner's Handbook*, it is noted that wolves require far more exercise than dogs, are more liable to develop territorial and pack behaviours and can seldom be trusted to behave gently around children and smaller animals. *The Conservationist's Guide to Wolves and Wolf Behaviours* states, rather more baldly, that keeping wolves as pets or working animals is effectively asking for trouble: *Captive wolves retain the instincts of their ancestors and will only display these tendencies more openly as they approach sexual maturity. It took ten thousand years of selective breeding to get dogs to do what we want. Wolves have spent the same amount of time living wild. You do the maths.* (*The Conservationist's Guide* is admittedly more upfront with its agenda than *The Ethical Pet Owner*.)

Of course, my Father's new wife was not keeping her wolf as a pet or a working animal, but rather as a daughter, which rendered much of the reading I did around the time of the wedding unnecessary. The day they moved in, she dressed the wolf in a blue pinafore dress she described as its *special occasions outfit* and presented me with a copy, in my size, which my Father suggested I change into before helping with the unpacking.

+

The wolf was named Helen, having been named after both Helen of Troy and St Helen of Constantinople, who reputedly discovered the true cross in Golgotha in AD 337. She was dust-coloured, slavered more or less constantly, which wasn't attractive, and had the other unfortunate habits of defecating in the corner of the kitchen and gnawing on table legs. In the early days of his second marriage, my Father took great pleasure in citing all of the literary precedents for her presence in our lives, although he owned that from Romulus and Remus to Mowgli, the more usual setup involved wolves adopting humans, not the other way around.

My Father's marriage upset the equilibrium – loosened the surety of my grip. My Stepmother, as I was requested to address her, unlocked windows, plugged mouseholes with wire mesh and foam insulation. The house opened around her the way you crack a chest cavity, the ribs of it, the unnatural gape. My Father and I had rarely felt the need to disturb things but my Stepmother moved in a sort of permanent sweep, gathering up my Father's shoes and papers and the glasses in my bedroom and scuttling them safely away. She was industrious, as I wrote to my sister: *she keeps things in the air.* She fed Helen three times a day with the kind of bottle you would give to a two-year-old child and read to her from history books she had brought with her from across the street. *Sounds exotic – best of luck,* my sister wrote, accompanied by a sketch of herself flying a kite with a tail of plaited ribbons. An inked-in sky, a navy afternoon.

My Stepmother took over the washing of my clothes, which I found I resented and combated by leaving dirty garments in places she couldn't reach like the top of the wardrobe or draped across the ceiling fan. I re-wore clothes until they came to smell like skin and itched unpleasantly, let my wrists and fingernails grow dark. What little dominion I had I maintained by making as much mess as possible. I balled up paper and threw it about without first having written on it, stacked up poltergeist towers of books. I stamped down the bin in my room until it burst with cotton wool, plucked hairs and soiled tissues, hung crusty skirts and blouses on the backs of chairs like sails. Every afternoon at three, my Stepmother came around with a brush and hoover to blast away this overflow, collecting and dispersing great menageries of garbage: dead violets, blunted lipsticks, forks and plastic beakers, nail clippings, earrings, half-eaten tins of peaches left to rot in my bed. That she did this with alarmingly good grace did not escape my notice, though my response to this was only to try harder, smearing jam from strawberry doughnuts on my bedroom windowpanes. *Little savage*, my Father said, in a tone that implied only anthropological interest, making a neat note in one of the books in which he stored ideas for future novels. Admittedly, I really ought to have outgrown this kind of behaviour. In a letter written lengthways on yellow legal paper, my sister wished me happy thirteenth birthday: *you're a grown girl now – for god's sake try to behave.*

+

The wolf was a novelty at first. On Saturdays, my Stepmother washed her in a large green basin which she kept beneath the sink in the kitchen and brought out with great ceremony, filling it first with hot water, then with cold water, then with a drop of vanilla essence and heavy lilac cream. I liked to watch this ritual sitting up at the kitchen table, peeling apples whose cores I would later spirit away and bury in my bedroom carpet until it smelled like sweat and stale sugar. My Stepmother washed Helen with a brush and pumice stone, mumbling Judy Collins lyrics and tutting whenever the wolf slipped out of her grasp and bit her. The biting was a frequent occurrence – the wolf was, after all, a wolf. By the time she had finished her scrubbing, my Stepmother would usually be bleeding gently into the bathwater and berating Helen for her attitude.

I had read in *The Conservationist's Guide* that the enforcement of unnatural doglike behaviours in domesticated wolves can cause distress and even trauma: *pet wolves, or what you might call wolfdogs, are liable to develop depressive and antisocial patterns when forced into systems of subservience that run counter to their instincts.* Of course, Helen was not treated like a dog, and her behaviour seemed roughly to correspond with her perceived status in the household. *Petted, rather than pet,* I wrote to my sister, referring to the way the wolf was strapped into a booster seat at mealtimes and fed apple sauce and gravy before my food was served. Her wardrobe was extensive and varied – my Stepmother had a particular fondness for dressing her in Tenniel bibs and dresses, pie-crust collars, yellow hats and lacy cotton boots. Her attitude was in some regards august, toothsome, more graceful than my own. She bit and scratched with impunity but seldom seemed unsettled or much inclined to escape.

One afternoon, as my Stepmother was just coming to the end of her bathing ritual, the telephone rang in the hallway. She had bound the wolf up in a towel the way she usually did and now passed this bundle to me without first asking, hurrying out of the kitchen before I had a chance to object.

I dropped the apple I had been coring, its streamer of peel uncoiling as it span away across the kitchen floor and disappeared beneath the fridge. Momentarily thrown, I adjusted the unexpected weight in my arms, abruptly aware of a smell which I had come to consider a general fact of the kitchen but which was, in fact, the wolf herself. The smell was fierce, a stifling of something thick and fleshy, dark meat beneath a slop of bluebell soap. *Feral smell*, I thought, before adjusting my vocabulary – *formerly feral*. My nostrils stung and I tipped my head away, squinting slightly as the trussed-up wolf wriggled up to face me, thick strings of dark saliva at her chin. For a moment, we blinked at each other – damp fur, a smell more like a temperature, straight slant of eyes unlike my own. She leant towards me, sniffed and briefly licked my teeth. In the hallway, I could hear my Stepmother talking loudly on the telephone. The wolf seemed to note this too, flicked her tail beneath the towel as though impatient and fastened lazy jaws around my chin.

The apple mouldered for seven weeks before my Stepmother found it, soft and hollowed out by ants which spilled from the dustpan she had thrust beneath the fridge in exploration, running up her wrists and biting at the skin beneath her sleeves.

+

At school, I told people my Stepmother had a daughter and no one questioned me because, for the most part, no one listened. I wasn't easy at school, grime beneath my collar.

Even before the divorce I had been a poor scholar, slow with mental maths and too sloppy to be trusted with a fountain pen. Classmates picked apart my walk, my ugly tennis shoes, the fact my Father wrote purportedly 'dirty books'. Boys with names like Callum and Jeremy made boorish jokes about my smelly clothing and the knots in my hair that resembled fists. *Pull her head back, dirty girls like it that way.* I spent a lot of time getting into fights, skinning my knuckles, the backs of my legs. Girls put chewing gum on my chair, pinched my sides when we clustered in the gym for assembly, sitting cross-legged and knee to knee. My sister, before she left, had been better with situations like this, had happily turned her nose up at people who laughed at her, never getting into fights. *Try harder*, she wrote, a dark dribble of words around a stick figure sitting upright at a cartoon desk, *don't be such a beast*.

I was fourteen when the wolf began to escape the house, walking the ten minutes between home and school to wait across the road from the netball courts until I emerged at four o'clock. The first time it happened, I only realised she was there because of the small crowd that had formed around her. A boy from the class below me had apparently tried to pet her and had immediately dissolved into hysterics when she bit him on the arm. By the time I arrived, his Mother had already broken up the tussle, leaping from the front seat of a stone-coloured Volvo to drag him away, still in tears and with a wad of tissues held to his wrist. Helen, apparently deaf to the uproar, perked up when she caught sight of me. She was clothed only simply, a small black cap and aproned pinafore that made her resemble nothing so much as a waitress at a casual restaurant. I held one hand out towards her and she pushed her snout between my fingers, licking at my dirty nails. The crowd around me pulsed – a mumbled curiosity. It was a Friday, a long time since her Saturday bath. I pressed my face into the protruding bones of her back and breathed her in. A smell like offal, like bone marrow beneath her dress. I elbowed my way through the crowd and she came with me, calm and slavering only lightly. We walked home together and I told her inconsequential things about my day.

After that, I found she came for me often, waiting patiently outside the school the way parents did, sometimes settling down with her chin on her paws, swatting her tail at horse-flies. My Stepmother, after her initial panic the first time she had found Helen missing, was surprisingly cheerful about the whole thing. *Nice to see you girls getting along*, she said, whilst my Father noted vaguely that it was preferable to letting me walk home alone.

+

We became friendly, if not to say filial. I took to brushing her fur until she bit me, fed her white rolls and anchovies until her stomach distended and she threw up on the dining-room floor. My Stepmother showed me how to bathe her on Saturday mornings, how to pumice the dead skin from the pads of her feet. *There's a girl*, was my Stepmother's most common refrain and one I found myself mimicking, soothing the wolf's irritation when filing down her claws.

I became familiar with the hunch of her body – the heavy ridge of spine and the way the fur became coarser towards the middle. Sometimes, sitting reading in the kitchen, I found she would clamber up beside me and turn pages at random with her tufted snout. Her smell varied, depending on the day of the week – fleshy, sharp, strangely vegetal. By degrees, I came to take an odd pleasure in mirroring her gestures, raising and lowering one shoulder, swallowing things without first chewing, drawing back my lips to expose the teeth.

She took to catching bats, at night in the midge-infested garden, bringing them in at peculiar hours and laying them at my feet. They were gory little offerings, dank-furred and often still twitching. My Stepmother disapproved and wouldn't let me keep them, scooping them up with her dust-pan and depositing them on my Father's compost heap. It wasn't ladylike behaviour, she said, though it wasn't clear whether her problem was with Helen catching the bats or my accepting them. I managed to rescue one, just once, sneaking out in an earthworm-scented dawn before my Stepmother woke and fishing the bat from beneath a pile of garden waste. I tried to dry it out beneath hardbacked books, the way my sister had taught me to do with flowers, and kept it the way I kept my letters, pushed down between the wall and the bed, until it came to smell so badly that my Stepmother found it and threw it away.

Sometimes, when the weather was cold, I slept with Helen in the room my Stepmother had set up for her, across the corridor from my own. She slept beneath a twin bed which my Stepmother made up neatly every morning, despite the fact the sheets were never slept in and the covers undisturbed. The smell beneath the bed was thick – body smell. I pressed my face each night into Helen's shoulders. She slept a jittery, doglike sleep, whined softly, snapped at nothing. I often imagined her dreams – subterranean, worm casts, a greenish undergrowth.

+

Whenever we had guests over, my Father would display Helen in her party dress – his exotic Stepdaughter, her interesting table manners. His friends were poets and visual artists, they asked my Stepmother serious questions about the urge to Motherhood. *Old as the earth*, a man who had once exhibited a series of photographs of undecorated driftwood informed her, swilling Côtes du Rhône, *the maternal desire, the natural order of things.*

My feral girls, my Father would say if Helen and I appeared together, pulling the wolf onto his lap and suggesting I sat at his feet – a broad artistic joke. I was older, taller than I had been. The middle and fourth fingers on both my hands had grown to the same length and my eyebrows met in the middle, which caused me less embarrassment than a certain sort of shifty release. The hair grew too fast to pluck and so I let it go and let my legs and armpits perform a similar trick.

At school, a girl who typically sat beside me in French class complained that I smelled and asked to be moved across the room. I continued to get into fights, although now when I did the teachers seemed less inclined to see my side of things.

At my Father's dinners, my Stepmother typically sat at his right and fed Helen with her serving spoon, leaning sideways to pass me pieces of meat from her plate. My Father served his guests a lot of salted beef, ox tongue, duck breasts still bloody in their jus. I liked his cooking more than I had in previous years, a fact which I owed both to the maturation of my palate and to the fact that meat, stolen away and buried in my bedclothes, settled down in time to a hard iron smell that I found I enjoyed very much. I had started my period on the evening of my fifteenth birthday and had eaten the steak my father served, near-raw, in a fit of jubilation. *There's a girl,* my Father had said, tipping the leftover juice from the grill pan onto my plate. Helen, who by this time was nearly out of adolescence, had sat by me through dinner in a muted splendour with a party hat cocked around her ears. It was at this dinner party, held in my honour, that a guest of my Father's – a renowned poet and radio philosopher – had caused a scene by knocking over the salt cellar and, in his haste to retrieve it, brushing his hand over Helen's flank. As she had with the boy outside my school, Helen had immediately locked her fangs around his wrist – not unpleasantly, but still enough to make him shout. My Father had laughed at this and reminded his guest not to upset his daughters, wiping his mouth with the back of his hand.

+

At the age of sixteen, I became of unexpected interest to a boy in my class named Peter who told various people he was in love with me and took to following me home at a distance of about a hundred yards when I left school for the day. The kind of boy who grows too fast and too abruptly over the summer and returns to school war-torn and alien, Peter was largely solitary; a characteristic which perhaps encouraged the misguided view that I had anything to offer him. The fact that, most afternoons, I had a wolf beside me during my walk home rendered Peter's omnipresence only nominally unsettling, though occasionally when I stopped, to tie a shoelace or to readjust my bag, he would stop too and only start again when I did. *That's boys for you*, my sister wrote on a postcard showing Raphael's *Annunciation, always on the horizon*. We hadn't spoken in a while and the cartoon in the corner of her message showed a girl rather taller than the ones she had previously drawn. It was standing with its hands behind its back, its hair demurely plaited down one side.

Helen was fully grown by this point and had long since lost her baby teeth. The process of losing them had been fractious, uneasy, a season of waking in the night to her dragging her jaw along the floorboards beside me until her teeth came away at the root. Her adult teeth were sharper, vampiric in a way my Stepmother regarded with concern, if not outward anxiety. Now and then, she presented Helen with tough things on which she was encouraged to gnaw – coconut shell and softened slabs of pumice, all the better to blunt her harsh new mouthful. Over time, Helen would grow bored of these objects and nudge them over to me. I would pick them up to make her happy, fit my teeth to the sides of a coconut shell and bite.

The Conservationist's Guide noted that wolves, at the point of sexual maturity, are liable to develop more alienating, predatory behaviours, and that domesticated wolves have a tendency either to draw away from their human companions or to become markedly more territorial around them. It was difficult to tell, at the time, whether either of these situations was particularly the case. By the time she had lost her baby teeth, Helen was not behaving notably differently to the way she had behaved before, although she did become more selective with the clothes in which she allowed my Stepmother to dress her and grew oddly snappish on the rare occasion I received a letter from my sister.

+

My Father published a new novel, dedicating it to me and to Helen, describing us as *my twin girls*. My Mother rang him up to berate him for leaving my sister out of the dedication. It was a Saturday, Helen's bathing day, and I listened to my Father's side of the argument from my seat on the kitchen floor. *It was your decision*, he said more than once, *you chose one and not the other. So did she.* Moving the pumice stone idly over the base of Helen's left forepaw, I thought about the evening my sister had packed her belongings, the expression like the cartoon girls she was so fond of sketching – flat and colourless, still-mouthed. *What do you expect*, my Father said repeatedly, *what do either of you expect.*

The phone call ended abruptly and my Father banged into the kitchen, pausing in what seemed like a high temper to observe the bathing ritual. Sitting patiently with her forepaws on the tub's edge, Helen cocked her head to one side and then the other, her ears today encased in a miniature yellow bathing cab which seemed to amuse my Father. He shook his head, moving across the room to a place on the counter where he kept family photographs and removing a snap of me and my sister at the ages of seven and eight from its frame. This he looked at for several moments before dropping it into Helen's bathwater as unconcernedly as one might stub out a cigarette. The photograph warped quickly in the soapy water and Helen dabbed at it unconcernedly, making no particular effort to rescue it before it sank. My Father moved out to the front of the house for some air, returning a half-hour later to relate in his novelist's voice that Mr Wintergarten had now moved on to kidnapping and stuffing neighbourhood cats, if the commotion from next door was anything to go by.

+

Walking home one afternoon, followed as usual by Peter, Helen took it into her head to butt at the backs of my knees until I understood her intention to change our usual route. I complied almost unthinkingly, crossing roads as she willed me and circling through unfamiliar streets, although at several points when I looked back, Peter was still following us and by the time we reached home, Helen was ill-tempered and flat about the ears.

At school, it occurred to me to confront him about following us, though when I did he only grinned and told me I should expect a certain level of interest if I would wander around with a wolf in tow. It was shortly after this that he started stealing pencils from my desk when he passed me to take his seat in the mornings, picking them up as casually as if he'd left them there for safekeeping. The third or fourth time this happened, I jumped up and snatched the offending item back before he could retreat to his desk. I opened my mouth to demand an explanation but found as I did so that the disparity between our heights made him somehow difficult to argue with, a shadow too long to entirely avoid.

+

The nights seemed larger by the age of sixteen, a curious sense that the strangulated skies of my childhood had suddenly been granted room to rage about. At full moon, Helen would go out into the garden and howl, the way that wolves are wont to do in movies, and she encouraged me to join her, dragging on my trouser legs until I accompanied her onto the lawn. Full-mooned nights brought with them a very particular ozone smell, a nitrous, liquid atmosphere that turned my hair to greasy curlicues. When she had howled her fill, Helen would prowl the garden in a strange, custodial circle, snapping at fireflies. *Did you girls have fun*, my Stepmother would ask us afterwards, sitting up at odd hours in the kitchen with her cup of orange tea.

You never write enough, my sister said – a cartoon of a girl, somewhat anachronistically, waiting by the telephone – *I feel like you're forgetting about me.* I wondered for a long time how to respond to this or to communicate the purge of her image that my Father had recently undertaken in all corners of the house. In the end, I filed the letter away like the others, pushing Helen's snout aside when she slunk up as if to read over my shoulder.

+

A month or so before my seventeenth birthday, I got into a fight at school. A group of boys with names like Callum and Jeremy had broken into my locker some time before the lunchtime bell and had swiped the box of tampons I kept hidden beneath a towel. The situation was a desperate one, an ooze and panic, dark smear along the back of my school skirt. I lined my underwear with thin school toilet paper, folded seven times, but the moment was torrential, hot fright between my legs, a spreading stain. At the end of the day, I sought out those I suspected, pushed Callum or Jeremy between the shoulder blades – stumble against the chain-link fence. We fought the way dogs do, open-mouthed, heads back and rearing. I smashed the heels of my fists upwards without looking, felt one connect – something wet and hard and quite like bone. Someone caught me in the side of the face with the corner of a schoolbag, an explosion like a hand driven into soft fruit, my vision sent marbling across the tarmac. I'm not sure how the fight ended, only that the crowd that had formed around us had dispersed by the time Helen found me and that I was alone when she did. She nosed into my side, licked one side of my face where something that had formerly felt solid now felt shaken loose. I found myself thinking of my sister's letter: *try harder, don't be such a beast.*

I had to fist my hands in Helen's fur to pull myself up, though she made no obvious objection. I caught something of my own smell mingled with hers, the dirt in my knees and the fact that between my legs I was still bleeding unchecked, a terrible falling away. We walked home together, a little laboriously, only stopping once when Helen tipped her head over her shoulder and I, following her gaze, saw that Peter was following us at his usual hundred-yard remove. I remember Helen lifted her head towards him, only a minor curl of her lip but enough to reveal the teeth, and he seemed to falter, before appearing to decide that this pause was invitation to move closer. He was, I saw as he approached, bearing the box of tampons that had gone missing from my locker, the ones I had assumed had been taken by the other boys. He raised his chin a little defiantly as he held them out towards me. *It was just meant to be a joke,* he said, his tone seeming to follow the set of his chin, though his words were nominally apologetic, *badly judged, had no idea. I didn't mean for it to get so out of hand.* Then a blur of action that was hard to follow – his hand passing over Helen's head in the way that she hated, the curl of her upper lip. Several weeks later, when he had been off from school long enough to make people curious, we heard that his hand had gone septic and that surgeons had ultimately had to remove the whole thing at the wrist.

+

In the aftermath of the incident with Peter, I went into my bedroom and found that Helen had ripped up all of my sister's letters and was sitting amongst the wreckage gently nosing her way through the shreds of cartoon girls, some stretching or skipping or bowling or rowing boats. I said nothing to this, only reached to stroke the hard, high ridge of her back, the familiar smell rising from her fur as I did so. Since the evening of the fight, when we had both returned home bloodied, my Stepmother had developed a habit of bathing me in the tub usually reserved for Helen and the scent of it – hot, bodily beneath bluebells – now seemed indivisible from the one I recognised as my own. Apparently satisfied, Helen turned to grate her jaw along the floorboards; a gesture like a sharpening – serrated knife against a block. The moon, I felt, was not yet full enough to excuse this kind of behaviour, but by degrees I nonetheless sat down beside my feral sister and joined her in dragging my teeth across the floor.

Stop your women's ears
with wax

1.

They wear glitter in Manchester – a queue like a Chinese dragon winding up past the traffic lights. Mona watches them hop from foot to foot, sharing chewing gum, straggle of autumn in their summer haircuts. Slips of chorus start and echo backwards, girls passing lyrics down the line. Finger-nails the colour of honeybees, bottom lips daubed with gold. *Barrier girls,* one of the roadies tells her, *they queue for hours just to get to the front.*

She takes her camera out to film short segments for the band's website. Three girls caught a bus at six this morning and have been hanging around the civic centre since nine. *It sounds extreme but we wouldn't do this for just any group, you know?* Further back, a gang of girls barely older than thirteen bare their teeth like knuckles and claw their fingers at the

79

lens. *We're the original fanclub. The OG. Other people say they started first but it was actually us. We liked them before it was cool.*

It starts to rain at six thirty – lurch of hoods and umbrellas. Those without are scooped sideways by companions, tucked under sleeves and into coat panels. The queue mutates into a travelling sideshow; two-headed girls in plastic macs, chimera-blooms of arms and hands as groups protect bareheaded members from the rain.

Doors at seven, mushroom of bodies. In the mirror-panelled foyer of the civic centre, they take photos of themselves in groups, sticking their tongues out. Hands are stamped and hip flasks confiscated – *No Alcohol Purchased Off The Premises* tacked at the foot of the stairs. Teenaged girls, tangle-handed, shoving through the inner doors. Melting nylon smell and anticipation sweaty at the upper lip, dark-ringed armpits – a keening, keeling, racing forward towards *the band the band the band*.

Later, back on the tour bus, Mona edits her footage together, intercutting her shots of the queue with sequences of the show and backstage. A tour diary, the management had requested, when they first took her on as video producer: *intimate access, behind-the-scenes, the fucking thrill of it all.*

On her laptop screen, Mona watches a clip of the evening's encore. The band – their long hair, their flaring nostrils – reappearing to the kind of clamour Mona has only ever seen reserved for the Beatles; weeping female fans in strips of documentary footage, fingers reaching up into eye sockets, digging down with a violence made slippery by tears. It is not a reaction she is used to seeing for a girl band. The scrabble, the sweat behind the knees. On the screen, she watches as the lead guitarist raises her hand for silence; a wide, extinguishing gesture which is swallowed up into the end of the clip. Skipping back, she watches again, focusing her attention on the audience before the shot cuts back to the stage. Pausing the video, she squints down towards the bottom left hand of the screen, noting two girls holding up a third who has fainted and now hangs between them, glitter-cheeked and livid to the lips.

2.

Liverpool – sticky-floored. There is some problem with the power distribution and Mona, the only member of the crew at a loose end, is dispatched to the venue manager's office to request a quick solution. *Nothing I can do, sweetheart, the building is what it is.* The office is papered with tour posters dating back to '72: The Who and Foreigner and ZZ Top. A clogged smell, sour towels and paper, a smell like overflow. The manager points to one poster and then another, *See these – see this one. Had them here in eighty-three. Power was enough for them it's enough for your lot, babydoll.*

The sound is bad that night, unbalanced; the bassist's amp keeps cutting out. Halfway through the set, the lead guitarist unplugs and walks offstage. The crowd heaves, a thrum like something under skin. Grief-stricken silence where a crowd might usually start to clamour, the audience clutching at each other, until the lead guitarist returns with an acoustic and an expression filled with teeth.

After the show, Mona revisits the venue manager's office to return the dressing-room key but finds the door bolted and the lock stuffed with orange thread. Scrabbling it out with a fingernail, she recognises it as the tangerine cotton from the band's T-shirts being sold in the foyer. She puts her eye to the keyhole and although she spies the shape of a figure in the office beyond, her calls elicit no response. Eventually she slips the key under the door.

That night, she goes for burgers with the road crew and sits in a vinyl booth stuck with chewing gum, Coke glasses sweating in the steam-heat coming off the industrial radiators. They are a close-knit company, a collection of women on the road, and their conversation is a pliant, textured thing, sympathetic to interruptions. They trade stories of when they first heard the band: *when I first got the call*, as someone says without irony. Catherine, the tour manager, spreads her hands across the table and affects a voice that holds a metaphorical torch beneath her chin: *I fell asleep on my sofa one night and when I woke up, their music was playing. Turns out, one of the music channels had started playing songs from their second album. Funny thing is, I could have sworn I'd turned the TV off . . .*

So you rolled over the remote in your sleep, the others laugh, though their raised eyebrows cover a rollcall of similar oddities: the wrong CDs in CD cases, the broken mirrors and messages written on steamed-up shower glass, the never-ending swooning, crooning sounds at night. In each case, they had been only miniature hauntings – whispered lyrics, songs playing on unplugged radios – but still enough to force them out onto the road. They press Mona for her story – *join the party, new girl* – but she demurs, picks at sweet-potato fries and folds her napkin lengthways. Later on, walking back to the bus, they make a game of reciting favourite lyrics, knitting words across words like a net beneath the tight-rope night.

3.

Road to York, two in the morning. Pulling over at Hartshead services, they wake to find the driver has opened the lug-gage hold and is ejecting stowaways. A twist of teenaged girls in orange T-shirts, chicken-skinned with cold. Cather-ine, hair stuck in the back of her sweater, gives them cab money and tells the girls to think of their mothers, how they must be worried sick. *Are the band on the bus?* one of the girls begs, staring up at the blacked-out windows. The band are in the back, as they always are, curtained off from the crew with a length of thick black serge – an unspoken *Do Not Disturb*. Catherine, of course, does not communicate this. *Don't do it*, says another of the girls, *you'll kill us if you send us away.*

*

Futile to go back to sleep. Mona sits at the front of the bus with the road crew and drinks coffee cut with rum. Someone is reading aloud from a day-old newspaper – venue manager from a previous city found asphyxiated in his office, clot of orange found halfway down his throat. They have all been sleeping badly, waking up sweating at strange hours of the night. Not so unusual on a tour, although perhaps odder that so many of them have been dreaming the same dreams; fractured thoughts of beating wings, of threads and electric weather, blasted motorways, pliant female skin and the sense of some unbearably beautiful song.

Ava, the black-haired roadie with the blue eyes, offers Mona a cigarette and they stand outside, kicking the tyres on the bus and comparing tour scars. Ava has a knot of displaced muscle in her left wrist from bending her hand back lifting an amp. Mona pulls up a crisp of hair from the place at her temple where she hit her head falling against the stage barriers whilst filming. *War wounds*, Ava grins, bumping knuckles in a gentle feint against Mona's chin. Her hand lingers, falls after a curious moment. She is taller than most of the women on the bus, swim-skinny, always overtired. When she exhales smoke, it is in an all at once sort of manner, a gust that briefly wreathes her head.

Back on the bus, Mona's sister rings and rings and she turns her phone over and ignores it until it finally vibrates itself off the table, at which point she turns it off.

4.

Silty air in Scarborough, a smell of burning when the bus pulls up short to avoid a motorbike.

The toilet on the tour bus clogs and they draw straws to see who has to fix it. The soundboard operator dredges up several yards of matted hair and a sticky black handful of feathers, which she wraps in tissue paper and throws out of the window.

Mona and Ava go for breakfast and sit in the café window, bleary with morning and three days of broken sleep. It has rained for the best part of a week – long squall, spongy asphalt – and the traffic is moving stickily at the intersection that borders the shopping precinct. They order eggs and buttered spinach and sit sipping at gritty coffee and attempting to recall the set list from the haze of last night in York. Ava ticks off songs on coffee stirrers, lays them down like dominoes, end to end. *'Black Chaos', 'Morgana', 'Apogee' – then something else.* Mona picks up the first coffee stirrer, moves it down the line. *They didn't play 'Black Chaos' first.*

She has noticed this before now, a tendency for the previous evening's show to fade from the memory, the smeared place where recollection should have been. It is a curious thing, a sensation not unlike surfacing from sleep and

85

grasping vainly for a fast-receding thought. It is as if she'll watch the show and then her mind will close around it, knuckle-clench the way a magician palms a coin, opens up with an empty hand. And yet every night, the feeling is clear: a rushing, wild euphoria. *You'll kill us if you send us away.*

At the intersection, a two-storey car-carrier pulls in between a Range Rover and an Audi with plush dice draped across the rear-view mirror. Tapping her fingers idly against the window, Mona watches the aquatic sway of the carrier as it rolls towards the lights, three cars strapped to its first platform and a further three strapped to its second. The rain has picked up again, gentle groan of coastal weather. At night, these past few days, the wind has been low, dragging its chin along the windows of the bus. Across the shopping precinct, she watches the grimy tumble of crisp packets, a blown-away umbrella. Ava is still lining up coffee stirrers, muttering song titles under her breath, and one of them sets Mona off humming – Ava grinning at her, joining in. They are almost at the chorus – an early song about breaking and mending, about hunger and revenge – when the car carrier, stalled at the lights, sways perceptibly in a fresh burst of wind. It is momentary, this queasy listing, but it is as the breeze dies that the backmost car on the carrier's second storey breaks its bonds and rolls gently off the platform, directly onto the Audi behind.

The cries are immediate, the clatter and spill. The waitress drops a tray of muffins as staff and customers stand and dash out of the café into the car park. Those who don't leave crush up against the windows, stand on chairs to get a better look. A swarming ghoulishness that couples with the horror of palms pressed to steaming glass.

Ava shakes her head, looks away from the sight of the crushed red Audi. Across the table, Mona taps her finger lightly on a hairline crack in the window, gaze towards the car but not quite on it, focus tightened on the glass beneath her hand. They rise to leave shortly afterwards, eggs and spinach both abandoned, turning away from the wreck as they exit the café. Knuckle-clench, the palming of a coin.

5.

Carlisle. Disorder. Mona films the queue outside the venue, watches as two girls in leather skirts go interminably over the moves of a secret handshake. They are stiff with hairspray, bare and tender at the arms. Tattoos of birds at their clavicles and up the backs of their legs. A group of seven or eight lead the line in a singalong, a tall girl in purple tights waving her arms in a gesture which mimics a conductor but more closely resembles the wielding of something blunt.

The night is wide, uncurving, like the earth might be flat and walkable from end to distant end. Mona watches girls nuzzle into the shoulders of their companions and tries to recall any instance of filming a boy in the queue. The band's audience, she knows, is broadly feminine – the kind of music that aches and claws its feet in bedclothes – but it occurs to her that there also isn't a single man in their crew. She powers down her camera, making for the back entrance. From somewhere inside, she hears the slight reverb of soundcheck, a swell of warmth within her like a welcome forcing open of her chest; the band's very particular wailing lushness, their wide and craving snarl.

6.

Hungover in Glasgow – braving the weather for bacon rolls. Sticky-faced and smeared at the lips with ketchup, the sound technicians trade stories about the fans. Making their eyes wide, flutter-fingered, fondly miming mania. *I remember once a girl snuck backstage by hiding in the band's laundry. I remember once a girl spent three days on the road with us by climbing into the belly of the drum.*

Exhausted, Mona feels brassy and nauseous, mustard on her shirt. Walking back to the bus, she has to sit down sharply on a low wall running parallel to the pavement. Ava pauses with her. Up ahead, she can still hear the sound technicians, now talking in carrying voices about the girls from Edinburgh and Derby, the girls in Hull who had been ejected from the venue and had scaled the walls to climb back in through a transom on the second floor. A story has been spinning about for several days about a group of girls in Keele who left the gig and holed up in a pub round the corner, drinking rum and Cokes and pints of shandied lager. Three hours later, they chased a boy out of the pub – chased him out into the road, so goes the story, straight into the path of a passing truck. *Knocked flat*, one of the sound technicians is saying, with a sound like blood on her tongue. *Exit pursued by barrier girls off their heads on lager and lime.*

The Glasgow venue is large and the get-in takes most of the morning. Mona tries to read on the tour bus but ends up falling asleep in her bunk and wakes to disorientating darkness, winter weather falling down in early afternoon. Smearing her face with clammy hands, she slides aside the cover on her bunk window and squints out over the car park. The back of the venue is just visible from this position and a queue of girls already snakes along the crowd barrier, hair dyed a number of frantic colours, like hybrid flowers bred into unusual shades. *Your core audience seems to be exclusively teenaged girls*, a recent magazine profile had noted, asking the band how they accounted for this bias. *Well why would there be anyone else*, the lead guitarist had replied, *you don't come to a party you weren't invited to.*

She sighs – so runs the rest of the article – and looks away from me. I am immediately made aware of my insignificance, as though the removal of her gaze from my person is tantamount to the removal of all gazes. Her bandmates follow suit and I am left like that, holding my Dictaphone up to the side view of three tilted (though still lovely) heads. A member of their management team appears from somewhere and I am informed in congenial doublespeak that the interview is over.

The road crew had read sections of the article aloud to each other. Congregating at the front of the bus, they had passed the magazine hand to hand and dripped disdain over its needling prose. *Hatchet job*, Catherine had fumed, while Allessandra from the lighting crew had kissed her own fingers at what she saw as a writer's punctured ego. *Their music is light, perhaps even frothy*, she had read aloud, *they are girl-pop's confessional figureheads, if not their leading lights.* Given only scant attention were the testimonials from fans, girls interviewed at shows and record signings: *They make music about yearning, about hunger. It's more than pop music, it's music that needs to ravage, to eat. Male bands are over. 'Boybands', I should say.*

Fucking rock journalists, Catherine had said later, *ought to have their fingers torn off.* From behind the black curtain at the back of the bus, there had come a sound rather like a laugh. Some weeks later, it was fleetingly reported in the same publication that the journalist would be taking an extended leave of absence due to illness and another writer was drafted to cover his regular slot.

7.

Mona spends the ferry to Belfast white to the eyeballs, vomiting over the side of the viewing deck. Ava brings her a flannel and a can of Diet Coke she bought from a vending machine that only takes euros. Mona wipes and sips and holds on to the lapels of Ava's jacket and ten minutes later they are pressed together on the galley steps, kissing with the acid zip of fizzy pop. Ava has hard hips, an easy manner, and afterwards says that the first time she heard the band was also the first time anyone kissed her. *I was seventeen, I think. Drove my brother to a house party I wasn't invited to. I let him out at the kerb and was going to drive right off but this song came on the radio and I ended up idling it out, having a cigarette. It was the second chorus when I realised a girl was climbing out of the upstairs window. One of his friends from the party. Shinning down the drainpipe. To get to me.*

They wander up to the ferry café and order tuna sandwiches and milky tea, sitting in a booth with their backs to the water and talking circles around the thing that just happened. The café deck is half-deserted, a smell of liniment and freeze-dried coffee. Along the far window, four of the sound technicians are curled up and sleeping uncomfortably on a long bank of metal seats. The band are not here. Mona had thought she saw the lead guitarist smoking a cigarette on the viewing deck when she first came out for air, although by the time she had finished throwing up there was no one to be seen.

Tell me how it happened, Ava asks at one point, pressing gently into her palm with three long fingers. *How you heard them first.* Mona shrugs as she replies. *Tell you about when I first 'got the call', you mean?* Ava rolls her eyes and Mona smiles at her, imagines sliding down a drainpipe to get into the passenger seat of her car – tug at her hair, irresistible. *Yes, the call*, Ava says, *the drag, the ache, the yearn, the need, whatever you want to call it.* Mona glances away, thinking of the road crew and the sound techs and the lighting riggers and all the girls who come to the shows every night with silver on the lids of their eyes. Beyond the windows, the water is pale and wintry, white surf like a kicking-up of snow. She shrugs again and gulps her tea and doesn't answer, thinking as she does so of the image it always conjures – the opened ribs, hands reaching into the pulp of her, a rhythmic movement of fingers, tapping out a song against her heart.

An announcement over the tannoy at twenty to one signals that passengers have ten minutes to return to their vehicles before docking in Belfast. Back on the bus, in the semi-dark of the car hold, Catherine confides what a member of ferry staff has told her: they are running a little behind schedule because a man had to be coaxed off the viewing deck, from which he had apparently been threatening to jump.

8.

Soundcheck in Galway – the band are bad-tempered, sing their songs as though being chased through them and ask repeatedly for alterations to be made to the sound balance, for the amps to be turned thirty degrees clockwise and the instruments to be moved to the left. Mona films the rehearsal, wondering idly as she does so whether half the footage will ever be used and what the point of it will be. At the edge of her shot, she watches Ava moving equipment, leaning up to adjust a spotlight, pale strip of twisting waist.

Catherine reports that the band seem better after sound-check, sitting in their dressing room eating grapefruit halves and fudge wrapped in strawberry cellophane. The general relief is palpable, as though the road crew's mood is hopelessly tied to that of the band. On the bus, the crew eat heavy noodles, fragrant with garlic, and Allessandra from the lighting crew reads tarot with grease-spotted cards. Curled up by the window, Mona picks the hanged man, the chariot and the nine of cups, although Catherine spills her noodles over the table before anyone can offer to interpret.

Later on, Ava and Mona wander down to watch the show. The music is liquid, drip-down – a sensation of something tarring their lungs, something fibrous caught between their lips. Afterwards, pushing out into the quiet evening, they tangle hands and Ava brackets her with pale arms, kisses her, a thrill like a fingertip to strings. They ditch the gig and get a hotel room, roll together through sheets chewed up with bleach. The room is arctic from the air-conditioning and Mona charts the quake of gooseflesh along Ava's arms and shoulders, follows freckles with an index finger and thumb. With her black hair and her bright white skin, she is soft, planetary, suddenly all illuminated. Burying her face in Ava's neck, she notes that there is an odd smell to her, a nervous-dog scent that thrills her. Their clothes lie puddled together on the carpet, two sets of skinny black jeans slithered out of like a tandem shedding. In the half light, they are both uncertain figures, luminous with bruises. They slot together quietly, a painful crook of fingers. Ava arches her back, eyes wide as a strangulation. Afterwards, they switch on the TV – a news piece about girls rioting in the streets near the venue. The sound is low, but the images lack nothing in clarity. A brief glint of video shows a crowd of girls flooding down the high street, bright with glitter and orange cotton T-shirts, breaking windows and throwing wide their arms. On screen, the moon is overlarge, stark and phosphorescent. It looms over the trampled high street, wall-eyed and gaping down upon the mess.

Mona's phone rings and rings – she doesn't answer it, only turning her head as Ava flicks the television onto mute. *I heard someone talking yesterday about a fan in Newcastle,* Ava says, *who brought some knitting to do in the queue before the show. Then later, when she left, she went two streets down to a bar she wasn't old enough to get into and drove a knitting needle through the bouncer's eye.* Mona shakes her head, mentally replaying her Newcastle footage – the long line of girls in neon trainers, perhaps some overlooked flash of needle points.

The stories are stranger here, or perhaps they are now simply far enough away from where they started to accept more outlandish versions of things they have heard before. A group of girls are said to have left the show in Hull and chased a forty-year-old man up a pylon. A girl in Nottingham is rumoured to have left the gig after the encore and returned

94

to her mother's house five hours later, holding something resembling a heart in her sticky fist.

Ava turns over onto her elbow and moves a hand down Mona's side, apparently done with talking. Mona allows herself to be pulled down and wrapped around with blankets, though she keeps her eye on the television and the long dark sweep of girls until the news piece is over.

9.

Early morning, at a rest stop outside Dublin. The company have disembarked to stretch their legs when Mona, doubling back to grab her wallet, comes just far enough along the aisle to see into the back, for once uncurtained. She can make out little, only Catherine stooped in rubber gloves, gathering up a matted nest of wide black feathers trampled down into the floor.

10.

Swansea, rain-glistered. Distracted, Mona picks up her phone without thinking and realises it is her mother too late to disconnect. The voice is flinted with distance, resentfully surprised. *I'd got so used to your voicemail.* The conversation lasts less than five minutes and holds the unpleasant timbre of a telling-off, though her mother quavers towards the end of certain sentences, as though her conviction is coming loose at one hinge. *It was unkind of you just to disappear like that,*

95

I don't care what the job is. I know it's work but to just up and leave everything – your whole life, with no warning – I'm sorry, I don't know. It just seemed unfair.

Afterwards, she walks down to the venue where the road crew are setting up. The queue is already tangled along the side of the building, more unruly than she has ever known it to be. The girls have overspilled the barriers and are pushing forward with unharnessed energy, jagger of voices like a hive held over a flame. The doorman presses a boot against the bottom of the door as it shuts behind her, testing the weight with the hobnailed edge of his heel.

The band have a live slot booked at a local radio station and the road crew play it over the PA system during set-up. The DJ is a middle-aged man with a drooping accent and a tendency to turn sentences down at the corners. *So tell us about your current tour,* he asks with an inflection like sending back soup at a restaurant, *I hear there's been some talk about your fans running a little wild – some bad behaviour, stunts out of hand and so on. Don't you feel that, as public figures – artists – you have some duty to your fans – many of them vulnerable girls – to set an example?* There is a crackle – thirteen solid seconds of dead air – before the lead guitarist replies: *Setting an example's all well and good but I personally wouldn't want the kind of fans who'd follow it. We just want fans who follow us.* The DJ seems to encounter some problem with his microphone shortly after that and the band obligingly step in to play an uninterrupted acoustic set that carries them into the four o'clock news.

11.

Ava asks if Mona'd like to get a hotel again when they get to Cardiff, sitting idle on the bus with her finger holding down the page of a book. They are all a little weary, undercaffein-ated. Two days ago, something had gone wrong with the coffee filter and they had barely realised in time that they'd all been filling up their mugs with blood. Mona drops down into the seat beside Ava, nodding vaguely and taking hold of her free hand. Catherine is walking up and down the aisle, stretching her legs in front of her and groaning as her knees and ankles crack. The lighting techs are playing canasta and drinking ginger beer at the table before the closed black curtain.

The bus rumbles around them, whirring on towards the next place as Ava reads and twists her fingers through the holes in Mona's jeans. Mona listens only vaguely, thinking back to her mother's phone call and wondering at the tone in her voice – tight, as if stretched thinly over something hidden. She tilts her head, trying to focus her mind on the decision she first made to follow the band, to really up and leave and join their crew. She remembers, of course, the first time hearing them, the opening sensation, the lurch. She closes her eyes, recalling the bloody little episode. Years ago, picnic blanket in her father's garage; the dust and daddy-long-legs and pulling up her shirt as the boy from across the road fid-dled with the radio. Something dour and masculine. *Listen to this one*, and biting her neck so hard her necklace broke

97

and spilled down between them. She had let him roll her over, moaned and writhed the way she knew she should, and then the music had changed to something else, channel changing unbidden to something vampish and inciting – coaxing fingers creeping out from the radio – and something inside her had smarted. Ribs, wrenching open, the sensation of something tugging on her spine, the wrong way, pulling out from the depths of her chest. Pushing him over onto his back, she had moved her hands up over his arms, over his chest and shoulders, coming to rest on his throat where she had fanned her fingers, pressed down until she felt something give. The music had bristled on into a chorus and she had leant forward as though sinking her shoulders into water, feeling the shape of her own mouth – at once soft and vicious, the prelude to a bite.

She remembers too the lack of afterwards, the nothing space of in between that became each gap between one song and another, each wait between playing a CD and getting to play it again, each year between first hearing them and finally joining them on the road.

When they arrive, the fans are already there, despite the fact the show is not for seven hours. The venue is ringed with frosted windows and the girls are pressed to the glass in great gangs, choking up the street. A local newspaper, it is soon discovered, has reprinted an old interview with the band as press for their arrival. *What are you?* the journalist asks at one point, going on to clarify that he just means to enquire what kind of genre they see themselves in: *rock, pop, indie, all of the above.*

Much later, Mona is dispatched to the dressing room to fetch the band for soundcheck and briefly catches the lead guitarist without her face on. She has forgotten to knock but thankfully no one sees her pressing the door open; tall sweep of wet black feathers. The face – the brief glimpse that she has of it – is a curious thing, familiar yet misplaced with its upturned nose and silvered eyelids, hanging over the back of a swivel chair.

12.

London at last. The driver angles the bus through a road gagged with girls who beat on its sides with the flats of their hands.

The venue is a large white oval building, a pitted eye lidded with tall gates which the girls try to climb. The crew hide the bus in the back lot out of sight of the road and slump down in their seats, considering. They are all hungry, white-gummed and bloodless. All of the freshly bought food on the bus rotted overnight and Catherine had to scoop it up into a plastic bucket, tipping it over the crash barrier on a layby.

They do the get-in quietly, a smell like pennies on the backs of their hands. The venue is a five-thousand-seater and the soundboard operator is worried about levels. *It won't reach the back row, people won't hear them.* Catherine shakes her head, still grimy at the fingertips. *Never been a problem being heard before.* Mona films the setup; the lighting technicians levering themselves up into the rafters like ragged birds with women's heads. On the stage, the road crew are arguing – a gentle sound, merely drifting. She focuses her lens on Ava, oddly veinless, the thin white lines at her temples.

There is a chip shop across the road and they send her out at five o'clock to fetch something resembling supper, passing unnoticed amongst the girls who throng the road. The boy behind the counter can't be more than eighteen, skin like fork-clawed cottage cheese. He eyes her curiously – the peek of her pass on a chain, tide of travel scum at her jawline – asks if she's working the venue tonight. *Who's the band*, he queries without inflection, and she tells him with a note of pride which crests and breaks against the dam of his indifference. *Oh, right, I think my sister likes them.* She sets her mouth in a line, pays him without thanks.

Doors at seven thirty. Mona is sent to film the band walking from their dressing room to the stage. The dressing room – what little she sees of it before the door swings shut – is a dark disaster, blackened stains on unforgiving surfaces. The smell is strong, a rotting like the peeling-off of flesh. In the dark of the wings, she watches the band through her camera display, registering as she does so a sensation quite like love, white-hot, devoid of logic. The lead guitarist grasps the bassist's hand, the rhythm guitarist pushes her fingers into her temples, holding the corners of something in place. From backstage, Mona films the roar of the crowd as the band passes out onto the stage. A sea of orange shirts and upturned faces, girls crying, already mouthing the words. Behind her in the wings, Ava rests her chin on her shoulder, watches the crowd through the camera display. *I love this song*, she says, anticipating. They stand there together as the lead guitarist strikes her first chord, both registering the same internal twinge, the vibrant, violent pulling.

On the news later, a brief video package, girls bursting from the venue and howling across the street. The velvet rage of their small mouths, hair torn from temples. A swollen werewolf moon. Orange T-shirts fraying at the hems, unwound and ragged. In a blurry clip, one can just make out the boy in the chip-shop window, the way he moves his hands up at the breaking of the frontage glass. In a thick swathe, the girls reach out for him, grabbing at his legs and neck and elbows, pulling him out through the window. The clip ends shortly after that, before the screaming and the rending, the camera swinging away to capture the mass of a thousand girls all racing forward down the street, the crooked note of music in the air.

Granite

There is no way to love a man. Not well, or rather, not correctly.

Maggie knows this and loves him anyway – a vast stupidity of love that a part of her views with a painful sort of irony. *Of course you love him, you fool, you idiot. What an utterly moronic thing to go and do.*

Her friends are nurses, midwives, physical therapists. They discuss the issue with clinical focus over Chenin blanc and Twiglets. Men, they say, are not built to withstand the same internal pressures. You can see it in their hips, the way they breathe after running. A lack in anatomical endurance. From a purely physical perspective, it is hard to love a man without breaking him apart.

Her friends have husbands, speak on good authority. She is late to the party, almost thirty years old.

'It's a design flaw,' they tell her, refilling her glass, a novice before the collective. 'Not their fault, exactly. Isn't to say that you *can't* love them, just that you have to be careful doing it.'

They show her photographs on their phones – smiling men, ordinary in earth-tones and morning suits – the men they have married and branded and kept for themselves. To her eyes, there is nothing obviously wrong with any of them; they all wear logo T-shirts, like to pose next to barbecues, all seem partially blinded by the sun. Her friends, however, tap their screens to zoom in on throats and the corners of eyelids, reminding her that to love a man is to watch him buckle. She comes away drunk and weaving slightly, catching her heels in the down escalator on the Tube. Her friends text her later, to ensure she got home OK, reminding her to be careful how she goes.

We're glad you're happy, Maggie – messages like little stones thrown into water, insincere and easily dismissed.

+

He is tall in her tiny kitchen, autumnal in his work clothes. He works in horticulture, designing gardens for historic properties, and his body is a dense, outdoorsy object. Crisp-cold, tang of stone and mineral, the bonfire sweetness when she kisses his cheek.

She thinks about him all day at work, answering calls with his voice caught up in her intonation. Picking compulsively at her cuticles, doodling his name in the claims forms and ripping them up to ensure that no one sees. Once, she forgets, fills in an entire sheet with his name, address and telephone number and posts it as internal mail, so that two days later he starts getting calls about his non-existent insurance claim and she has to speak to customer services.

'Clerical error,' she tells them and imagines them seeing through to the inner mess of her, though in reality she is only asked not to make everyone's job harder by being slipshod with her own.

Coming home, she picks up supermarket wine and stupid canapés – prawn mousse on scallop shells, Jerusalem artichoke crisps. He usually cooks dinner but she likes to contribute something, to pass him something on a plate and watch him eat it. The journey home has been transformed, a surprisingly luxurious thing. On the Tube, her carrier bags bump against her ankles; the crush, the tinny overspill of other people's music; yet all of this is now somehow part of a larger picture. Changing lines, an assault of elbows, doors closing on the edge of her sleeve; and yet anticipation like something worn about the shoulders, impervious to all discomfort.

In her flat, the charm of his bare feet on her floorboards. Stooping to kiss her, holding his hands away from her sides.

'Don't touch me, Mag, I'm covered in garlic.'

'I wasn't going to touch you. Why would I touch you? I don't know where you've been.'

She kisses him again like that, holding her hands away in mimicry; half-notion of a game for later. He quirks an eyebrow at her and she pulls away, pours two glasses of wine.

He cooks because he is better at it. He understands which

flavours go together, how to time things so that nothing burns. She clowns to cover her comparative uselessness, serves her pre-bought canapés with exaggerated flourish – blinis plated in concentric circles, dates split lengthways and piled with Shropshire Blue.

'Imagine if I could actually cook,' she says, offering up a devilled egg between pursed fingers. 'What a catch I'd be.'

'Triple threat,' he agrees. 'Singing, dancing, cordon bleu.'

'Probably just as well I have a flaw,' she nods, watching him edge a saucepan of something fragrant off the heat, the dark breadth of him beneath the strip light. 'Makes me more human, don't you think?'

Over dinner, he tells her a story about an argument he had with a client, the owner of some twenty acres of parkland who wanted the centrepiece on a restored sculpture fountain done in an inferior granite rather than marble, to keep expenses down. Later, he scrubs his hands to rid them of the garlic and pulls her to him with his fingers still wet, hard at the tips and oddly gritty.

+

They had met at a birthday party for someone her friends had been hoping she would marry. A stupid sort of day, insincere with sunshine. She had sat on the patio steps and watched people she didn't know eating mozzarella and beef tomatoes, bacon-wrapped chicken, sugar-dusted doughnuts and Comice pears. Thelonious Monk playing on someone's speakers, ''Round Midnight' at two o'clock in the afternoon.

Her main impression of the person she had been dragged there to meet was that he was very loud and welcoming and she couldn't wait for him to go away. He had shown her his collection of branded shot glasses from his trip around America and she had nodded and finished her drink too quickly, spilling, seethe of tonic water over her wrists.

In the past, her friends had accused her of being picky. Rolled their eyes at her inability to overlook a bad shirt, asked gently if she thought she was so very perfect herself.

'No sense wishing,' they would say, weary when she found a man dull or difficult. 'Maybe you're better off without.'

She would agree with them, of course – frank feminist, happy with her job and her hobbies, easy in her single skin. Privately, however, she knew herself better. Knew herself for what she was: a great failure at solitude. Sluicing through her twenties illuminated only by the glow of terrestrial television, finding much to her dismay at the age of twenty-nine that she longed to amuse and to be longed for. A faint life. Eating apricots and growing bony and forgetting how to talk to people. Loneliness like a taste on the skin.

He had turned up late to the party, too tall in the patio doorway, bumping his head on the lintel. Gentle touch of his hand. A relief great enough to change the very music on the speakers: Thelonious Monk cycling through to 'Werewolves of London' by Warren Zevon. Whoever had made the playlist clearly hadn't given much thought to the importance of segue.

+

Her flat came ready-furnished and the wallpaper is the colour of veal – overcooked and slightly sickly, the same colour which has seeped into the carpet and the curtains, the counterpane on the bed. In the mornings, his right thigh makes a clicking sound like the resettling of a bone in its socket. His groan, a painful satisfaction. Lifting his arms above his head to snap his shoulders into place.

As a boy, so he tells her, his mother would insist that cracking his knuckles would lead to arthritis. Reading aloud to him from *Mary Poppins*, his mother would place particular emphasis on the character of Mrs Corry; the woman with the barley-sugar fingers who snapped them off for other people to eat.

'There was a lesson in that for me somewhere,' he reflects. 'Though it mostly just made me bite my nails.'

Clouded with morning, his body is a curious jigsaw. She takes his fingers and kisses them, mimes a bite to the tip of his thumb.

She usually showers before sleeping and overnight her hair dries into ridiculous contours, pale blonde and fluffy with static from her percale sheets. She jokes about her hair having a life of its own and he tugs gently at it, pulls his hand away in a mime of alarm.

'Something bit me!'

'You think you're so funny.'

Mornings have been the hardest things to adapt to; company after three decades of waking up alone. She has always considered herself the kind of person seen to best effect at four p.m., once the day has burnt away and softened up her difficulties. Having someone with her from the outset gives her no rehearsal space, no time to sink down into some more pliable version of the creature she is to begin with.

'I like quiet in the mornings,' she had told him once, pressing a hand to his mouth before he was properly conscious so that he had woken up blinking rapidly and thinking he was being attacked.

Once he had understood her, he had done as she asked, dressing with his tongue between his teeth, and she had found herself talking to him anyway. Holding up two shirts and asking for an opinion, catching his eye in the mirror and feeling guilty as he mimed incapability, a stitched-up voodoo mouth.

'You can talk,' she had said at last. 'I'm sorry.'

Pulling invisible threads from his lips, dragging out his voice like something caught in a net.

He leaves earlier than she does, pulling on his wax jacket and his backpack, too tall for her without her shoes. On the way out, she hears him calling good morning to her elderly neighbour, Mrs Lumis, who occupies the basement flat and has taken to loitering in the corridor to tell him he has no business messing with lonely girls.

'Don't think I don't see you, my lad. You think you can move about beneath my notice but I see what you do. Watch your step. Mind your feet.'

'I will, Mrs Lumis. I've got my walking boots on.'

In the fifteen minutes after he leaves, the relief of space

falls flush against the greater relief of missing him. Maggie tames her hair with pins, lipsticks her mouth. Leaving for work, she finds Mrs Lumis still in the hallway, waiting to fix her with a wounded look and call her 'Margaret', which is not her given name.

'It's *Maggie*, Mrs Lumis. Just Maggie. You know, we don't need to be so formal with each other. We've been neighbours for two years.'

Mrs Lumis stares at her – wraithish figure in the corridor, as though the dust from all the unswept corners has been thrown by some disturbance into brief corporeality. She is a sore-boned woman, grimly hyaline, wigged to cover the bald head that Maggie has glimpsed occasionally – pale through the basement window bars.

'Your visitor slams doors,' her voice like a path picked through glass. 'All night the noise. Slamming and footsteps. Stops me sleeping.'

'I'm sorry if he does,' Maggie replies, unaccountably depressed by the droop of Mrs Lumis' wrists, eggskin sliver of white between her nose and upper lip. In recent weeks, Mrs Lumis's eyes have started losing colour at their centres. Maggie imagines the morning crusts at the corners of her eyelids as flecks of iris that have leaked out in the night. 'I have to go to work now but I'll talk to him about it.'

'You needn't do that.' Mrs Lumis speaks quickly, the scrambling fright of someone caught in a lie. 'Just don't have him here any more, then he won't have doors to slam.'

'I don't think—'

'Better for everyone,' Mrs Lumis barrels on, face set with some unpleasant meaning, 'in the long run. Better for him to not be here.'

Maggie looks at her, at the rubbed-off corners of her lonely body, and registers a certain pricking horror. A hot, unsettled recognition. All the way to work she feels it, needles in the hollows of her feet.

+

Morning sky, gasp of purple, like the dark part at the back of a throat. Day like a swallow. Promise of snow.

A chilly sliver of floor. She picks barefoot across the kitchen to gather coffee, croissants warmed in the oven. She piles a tray with milk and butter knives, honey and apricot jam. Thinks about it for a second and then forces open the frosted kitchen window, pulling a spray of winter cyclamen from the planter outside. This she arranges in a water glass beside the coffee press, standing anxiously back to assess the effect. On impulse, she pulls the flowers from the glass and tucks them behind her ear. Thinks better of it and returns them to the glass again.

'You have a wet ear,' he says when she brings in the tray. His voice is bad today, gravelled with cold, and as she clambers in beside him he turns away from her to sneeze. She has a funny impulse to kiss him then, to take his germs or whatever is wrong with him into herself on a long inhalation. A disgusting sort of perversion, love.

Her bedroom is warm, rat-king of tights on the dressing-table chair. His shoes are upside down and drying on the radiator. At work the previous day, he had turned his ankle on a patch of slate paving. The skin around the bone is already mottled, dark spread like a spilling, blue and grey.

'Better stay off your feet for the weekend,' she had said, waggling her eyebrows at him to make him laugh. He had stolen arnica from her bathroom cupboard to bring out the bruising, smell of antiseptic on his palms.

After coffee and croissants, he presses her down into the mattress. In her tenderised, meat-coloured room he holds her wrists together, bites her neck. Stone-weight of him, a reassuring breadth.

Later on, she goes back to the kitchen to wash up. Looking out into the shared garden, she sees Mrs Lumis making a shuffling tour of the lawn in the first of the snow. A strange sight, spectral. Like death walking in the morning, looking for its lost cat.

+

The key, she has been taught by the books she reads, is to love a man slightly less than he loves you. That way you remain in some sense unreachable. An inch above the floor.

It is the shape of his mouth that makes this impossible. The crest of freckles up his back. He sleeps as if murdered, as if set in concrete, flat out and immobile. On one of their first nights together, he had set seven alarms to go off at three-minute intervals and in the morning had slept through every one. She had lain there confused, dead man in her bed. Had realised that there could be no way of loving sensibly if every morning started with the relief of finding him still alive.

Her friends call him 'the gorgeous man'. Say it to his face sometimes, the way one might address a dog: 'And how is the gorgeous man today?' In meeting him, they seem collectively to have forgotten that they ever accused her of being fussy. 'Worth the wait,' they tell her smugly, as if the advice had been theirs, 'he's a paragon. Now for God's sake don't screw it up.'

+

The snow settles – city pressed in clay. You can feel the confusion, a tightening of formerly unsolid things. Ice on car windows, difficult breath.

His ankle has continued to trouble him, an irritation that lasts into the week. On the Wednesday, he rolls up his trouser leg and she sees that the bruise has blurred down into something stranger, greyer; an unexpected goriness that makes her bite her lip.

'Is it painful?' she asks, watching him hop about her kitchen, though he only shakes his head, chops onions, reaches for the salt.

'Not particularly. It's mostly just annoying.'

He tells her that when he was thirteen, he grew nine inches in the space of a summer and was barely able to walk. 'My mother called it the Bad Summer,' he says, gesturing to his hip. 'The tops of my legs kept popping out of their sockets because everything was growing too fast. She tells these stories about me falling down stairs because I couldn't get a measure of myself, these great piles of limbs she'd find everywhere. Like my body was coming apart or like something was trying to get out. It sounds brutal but honestly, I barely remember it now.'

She loves stories like this, loves to describe her childhood back to him, her own swift descent of stairs. Finding points of congruence is a never-ceasing fascination, the smells and morning newspapers and little superstitions that bridged their early lives, every similarity more meaningful than she knows it ought to be. In truth, of course, there is little correlation. He grew up further north than she did; a big house, an anthology of cousins, a string of dynastic family dogs. Her childhood was a smaller thing. Ugly duckling, her teeth birdcaged with braces. Barely five feet tall by the age of fifteen, she had spent her schooldays being left off netball teams, styling her hair to cover her face. Her mother, a narrow-lipped, resourceful woman, had told her at her university graduation that no one was going to marry her with a miserable face like that.

She likes to tell him things like this and watch his forehead contract as he tries and fails to picture it. In this way, she becomes aware of the curious history of the world, the wide gulfs of experience that can exist between lovers.

After dinner, they watch television and she takes his feet into her lap. In the dark, his skin has a blue tinge, as though it has been through the wash with a new pair of jeans. She rubs circles in his ankle with her thumb, frowning at the texture. The skin is dry beneath her fingers, a sensation like wax, like the breaking down of a doll.

+

It is easy enough, of course, to forget that she loves him. On the days between frenzies, when he leaves muddy footprints on the kitchen lino, when he whistles through his teeth. No one, she is sure, is capable of loving all the time, without interruptions or reprieves. Occasionally, there will simply be days when he smells wrong, when she thinks she spots something different inside him, and then she will push him away when he tries to kiss her, wipe her mouth with the back of her hand.

Sometimes, she fantasises that he has died. Died in some cinematic disaster; run down by a motorcycle, a clot on his lungs. In these dreams, she goes to his funeral in a Spanish mantilla and afterwards moves far away to a place where it rains. The fantasy is detailed, though changeable. She gets a job in a cafe or a cinema, learns to roast a chicken. Sometimes, she has his name tattooed on her ankle and sometimes she pierces her ears. Eventually, she moves in with some handsome local man with no passions and no interests who kisses well and doesn't need to be loved. They live together in the broad forgetful blue of this town, sharing nothing of themselves, perfectly happy.

The culmination of these fantasies always scares her and she finds herself calling him up at his house just to hear him, bleary and irritated at some throwaway hour of the night.

'I just called to say I love you,' she will say and he will tell her to stop quoting eighties pop music at him and to call him again at nine.

Her friends are impatient with her inconsistencies, tell her she is looking for excuses.

'You have what you wanted. Why pick holes in it?'

She tries to tell them that that isn't what she means to do. Sour with salted crisps and mulish at being, as she sees it, wilfully misunderstood. She leans forward over her knees and says again that she is happy with him, she isn't disputing that fact, but her friends only move the wine away from her and remind her of what she was like before he came along. 'Maybe you were alone too long to find it easy now, Maggie, but that shouldn't be an excuse.'

These lectures leave her feeling self-righteous, unfairly chastised. Coming home sticky-lipped from the wine and the argument, she will grumble and thrash her way through a solitary evening, watching television alone and ignoring her friends' messages, heating dinner in the microwave. She will canonise her former loneliness with a tang of self-pity, pretend to revel in the re-established silence, the remote control and sofa to herself. Before him, she had often wondered whether solitude was a skill one could lose like schoolgirl Latin, or whether it was simply a talent one acquired, bike-like, never afterwards forgotten. Now, of course, she knows her limits better. By the end of a single evening alone, she is usually sated. Calls him up to ask what he's up to and whether he wouldn't rather come and be with her.

+

Mrs Lumis is on the basement stairs without her wig, skunk-like in a balding housecoat. Maggie tries to get past without comment, but Mrs Lumis never emerges unless she has something to say.

'Your visitor was at it again – all night the slamming and the crashing. Rockslides through my ceiling. Not a wink of sleep.'

'He really wasn't, Mrs Lumis.' Maggie is tired, carrying Chinese food that is burning through her shirt. 'We went to bed at nine thirty. He doesn't get up in the night.'

Mrs Lumis shakes her head and Maggie finds herself guiltily transfixed by the eggcup curve of her skull. She thinks of the box of wigs with which her mother had once encouraged her to play dress-up – imagines herself fitting polyester hair to her neighbour's head; the bobbed red wig, the sleek Elvira.

'Better to send him away, with all that banging,' Mrs Lumis continues. 'Doesn't suit it here. Better to send him off.'

Maggie is distracted, eager to get upstairs.

'If you are hearing anything, Mrs Lumis, I can promise you it isn't him. Maybe we have a ghost.' *Or maybe you're making it up*, she doesn't quite say, only hiking the bag of Chinese food higher up her chest.

Mrs Lumis shakes her head.

'No ghosts, dear. Just you and me and him.'

She escapes without good manners, gesturing to her food

in half-apology and staggering backwards up the steps. She finds him in her kitchen, awkwardly collecting up pieces of a bowl he has apparently just smashed.

'And I told Mrs Lumis you *weren't* the one making noise,' she sighs, putting down her Chinese food and crouching to help him, swatting his apologies away. The bowl is glazed blue pottery, a tourist purchase from a week in Stoke, and he pieces it back together with a sweet precision, promising to find some glue. She pulls his hands away, already laughing, though the shock of his fingers is enough to blunt her smile. He is cold, even for a chilly evening, and she quickly sets him to unpacking the hot plastic tubs of beef chow mein.

He has been off work the past couple of days at her insistence. His ankle is worse and frustrating him and his cold seems no better. At night, his breathing is difficult, a crumbling thing, like a flaking off of paint. He tells her, shrugging, that he had pneumonia as a boy and is simply more susceptible to cold and flu, though his shrug makes such a blur of cracking noises that she is almost too distracted to respond.

'You shouldn't work outside,' she tells him later, eating sesame noodles on the sofa and drawing distracted circles in his leg. Propped on the coffee table, his feet are white and bloodless, a peculiar beating of his pulse high up in his knees. 'Not in the snow, anyway. Not in weather like this.'

'Got to earn my filthy lucre,' he replies, nudging her hand deliberately off his leg. 'Keep you in a manner to which you're accustomed.'

It is a joke, though a weary one, and he yawns right through its middle in a way which messes up the tone. Rolling his shoulder – another fluster of splintering sounds – he slides further down the sofa. A banging sound starts up, noise like pipes thumping up through the floorboards, and it takes Maggie several moments to realise that Mrs Lumis is beating at her ceiling with something like a broomstick. A rhythmic imperative – *get out.*

+

The first time they had slept together had also been the first time. She has never told anybody this; she is, after all, practically thirty.

She had bled, of course, and passed it off as her period – *talk about bad timing* – a nervous snort of a laugh. He had ignored this, kissed her chin and eased her over onto her side, and she had loved him then about as much as she ever would come to later, loved him for the ache of his kindness and the things he chose not to see.

The pain had been worse than expected, though not in the way she had imagined it might hurt. She had always pictured men battering away at her; a great internal shearing, a falling all to bits. In truth, of course, it was all very much as her most honest friends had assured her – ineffably more boring and more enjoyable, the pain sharper and more localised; egg crack against the rim of a bowl.

Afterwards, he had not smoked a cigarette or talked or tried to hold her, only fallen asleep for a curious half hour and then woken again, asking whether he had been snoring.

Pale man in her meat-coloured bedroom, long blue eyes and his smell like grass and eiderdown and something stranger; damp down a wall. Looking at him then, she had thought about all the men who might have preceded him, the men she had allowed to take her out to movies and sit-down dinners but forestalled before letting them into her flat. Always a reason, of course; a stupid comment or a quick flash of violence, a seam of cruelty in some region of their bodies (a grabbing hand, a dark and fleshy underside). Enough, whatever the reason, to make her wish to bar their way any further, to invent excuses and take the train back home alone.

'There's always *something* with you,' her friends had said to her. 'Always something with any man you meet. It's like you don't want a man at all, you want an object. Something you can put away.'

In truth, she had often wondered whether the problem was actually her – whether she brought out the monsters in them. By logic alone, after all, they couldn't all be as dreadful as they seemed when she got to know them, or else why would anyone marry them, want to have them near? *Prolonged contact*, she had reasoned when slick with Chardonnay, deep in self-pitying vein, *that must be it. Too long with me and they all turn, become worse.*

That first night with him, she had watched for the change. A shifting in aspect, a re-carving of the bones in his face. She has watched for it every night since, that sudden monstering, but so far has found nothing. Perhaps, she hopes, whatever power she has is waning. Perhaps she can control it with a man she loves.

+

'Look at this.'

She is brushing her hair in the dressing-table mirror. Wide yawn of morning. The snow is packed tight outside, soft pulse like the struggle of bound wings.

Still looking in the mirror, she sees him holding up his hands. The skin around his fingernails is mottled dark, as though he has soaked his hands in vinegar. As she watches, he rubs one wrist against the other, a strange solidity of movement, rattle as of something thrown. In the foxed glass, there seems little delineation between his fingers. They bunch together stiffly, unyielding and brittle as handfuls of cutlery.

'What is that?' she asks. 'Chilblains?'

'I don't know,' he replies. 'Must be. This weather.'

'You have to keep warm,' she says, biting her lip as he catches her eye in the mirror. 'You never wear socks.'

'Not on my hands, no.'

'Not on your *feet* either. It's not funny. This is why you're always catching colds.'

He nods, crossing the floor to press a placating kiss to her head, shooting her reflection a smile which she does not return. Her hair has turned to straw in the cold weather and she yanks hard at a snarl. Sharp split of pain.

+

In the kitchen, she pieces the blue bowl back together with superglue and watches Mrs Lumis from the window. Her neighbour is making her customary tour of the garden, though the snow is now knee-deep in some places and unpleasantly gritty besides. It has been a strange week, inconstant with its light and with its timings. Long afternoons stem from mornings passed in the tilt of an egg timer, whilst an hour of every night seems to last its own century, whole epochs dragged out in stubborn wakefulness and his painful breathing on the left side of the bed.

Thick with flu, he has stayed the week more or less involuntarily. She has piled him with duvets and is keeping him what she fears might appear a sort of prisoner, though he has stopped protesting since he lost the feeling in his feet.

'Very *Misery*,' he had joked weakly, in response to her first assault on the bedroom with soup and ginger ale, though he has since grown sleepier and less prone to comment. In response, she had thought to say something light-hearted about being his number-one fan, though it had occurred to her just in time that such a comment might be taken as more threatening than it was meant.

The snow has packed the city so densely that nothing can be moved. There is no work to go to – no trains, no buses – and streetlights go down intermittently at night.

Standing by the kitchen window, Maggie holds the bowl in cupped hands to speed the glue's drying. In the garden, Mrs Lumis has paused in her rotation and is inspecting a seemingly unremarkable patch of snow. She is wigless again today, although Maggie is oddly relieved to note that she has at least chosen to wind a scarf around her head. The woollen tassels at each end hang down like a mime of hair, little coils of green angora fringing the back of her neck. Watching at the window, Maggie finds herself thinking of a story her mother used to tell her, about an old lady who had lived alone in their street for seventy years, before finally being found desiccated in the pantry, having fallen and apparently been pickled by the fumes from an open drum of vinegar she kept there for fixing preserves. For her part, Maggie had always found it a little unfair that her mother should encourage her to be fiercely independent, whilst also making a horror story out of being alone.

Later, once she has shelved the mended bowl, Maggie goes back to the bedroom and slips under the covers, curling into his side in the way she has become used to, fitting her feet to the backs of his knees. His hands, when she touches them, are heavy and strange and he mumbles to her about barley sugar. Drifting in and out of sleep, she thinks of hibernation, of things that turn hard and chrysalise as a way of surviving the cold.

+

The first time they met, he had handed her a beer with his thumb pressed to the top of the bottle, to prevent it fizzing over her dress.

'So, what's wrong with you?' she had asked him. 'Why are you single?'

He had laughed, cracking reflexively at his knuckles, and asked what was wrong with her.

'Make a list,' she had shrugged. 'Bitch, gorgon. I'm difficult.'

'Says who?'

'Me, mostly. My friends say I put people off.'

Her friends had warned her against throwing herself too rashly at a man she knew nothing about. 'Don't put your eggs in one basket,' they had counselled. 'You know how easily disappointed you can be.' Of course, since these were the same friends who had variously advised her never to love a man but still to find a man, to settle for a man, to wait for perfection, to move on and change the subject, she had ultimately ignored them all, swanned her neck and fallen for him anyway.

The first time he had stayed over, Mrs Lumis had emerged from the basement in the tight blue morning when Maggie was coming down to fetch the newspapers.

'New man,' Mrs Lumis had said, and Maggie had been surprised by her, lopsided in her white-blonde wig. 'Something wrong?'

'What? No, nothing's wrong. Long time no see, Mrs Lumis. I thought maybe you'd moved out and left me.'

Mrs Lumis had said nothing to this, only pulling a tragic expression that Maggie had found somehow grotesque and looking up towards the stairs.

'Difficult,' she had said, apparently to herself. 'Trying to keep a man. Always safer not to look directly at them.'

+

She wakes, as usual, to one of his alarms. He, as usual, does not.

The morning is still dark beyond the curtains, snow-dark, a crust of rime about its edges. Freeze-bite before a thaw.

'How are you feeling?'

Moving slowly, still bleary from a cold and shifting sleep, she presses her legs against his, makes to warm her feet against his ankles. A strange sensation. She blinks. The bed-clothes are cool around him, heavy object wrapped in cloth.

Leaning up on one elbow, she touches his shoulder, tries to brush his hair from his eyes and meets resistance. Clink like china. The light is bad, too chilly for any clarity, though from what little she can see, it seems that something is wrong with his face.

She says his name, touches his wrist. A feeling like fingers pressed to a wall. He is hard stone, though not quite marble. Something granular – granite or porous limestone. Dark gravity in the left side of her bed.

She tries to hold him, but the stone is coarse, untreated. He starts to come apart in her hands.

Smack

The jellyfish come with the morning – a great beaching, bodies black on sand. The ocean empties, a thousand dead and dying invertebrates, jungled tentacles and fine, fragile membranes blanketing the shore two miles in each direction. They are translucent, almost spectral, as though the sea has exorcised its ghosts. Drowned in air, they break apart and bleed their interiors. A saturation, leeching down into the earth.

People claim they are poisonous – Sea Nettles, Lion's Mane, Portuguese Man of War. Bringing their phones down to the beach, they snap pictures, send them into nature shows. One photograph makes it into the local paper, another fills five minutes on a regional morning show: *'And in local news, a shoal of jellyfish has been causing consternation for tourists at one of the more popular pleasure beaches. Certainly not what you'd expect, coming up for a long weekend, is it, Cathy?' – 'Actually, Tim, I think you'll find a group of jellyfish is called a "smack".'*

The provenance of the jellyfish remains a mystery. People argue amongst themselves, message links to articles back and forth. They are the result of global warming, of toxic-waste disposal. They are a sign of a change in worldwide migration patterns, rising sea levels, El Niño. They are Californian and a long way from home.

From the back porch, Nicola watches the clean-up for the best part of the afternoon. She has been in her dressing gown since the previous evening, sharp with yesterday's deodorant, caking of toothpaste in the corners of her mouth. She watches men with rubber shoes and litter-pickers moving down the beach, scooping up the glutinous shapes with pails and trenching shovels, dumping them down. The day is hot – white summer, restless with foreign birds. On the deck, she sits with one ankle hooked over the other and eats croissants, stale since Tuesday morning, slugging coffee black because the milk has turned to yellow curds.

Beneath her dressing gown, she is bloody with mosquito bites. Unrazored beneath the arms, unplucked, unmoisturised. The yeasty smell of unwashed bedlinen, salve on childish bruises. Last night, she ate outside – pre-cooked garlic prawns, torn from the packet – and the plates have been left to moulder in the heat of the day. Vulture-like, gulls circle the deck. Dark wails across a melted sky.

'You'd set yourself on fire, if you ever tried to live by yourself,' Cece had once said. 'Two days, tops. You'd boil an egg and burn the kitchen to the ground. Either that or we'd find you three weeks later, suffocated under piles of your own mess. You're not a natural housekeeper, sweetie. You're not that type.'

'Only because you've never let me try.'

Cece's expression – sag of irritated eyes.

'Any time you want to, sweetie. You just be my guest.'

Her phone has been dead since the weekend. A blessing, in many ways. The power in the house is off, has been off since she arrived, and she has no idea how to turn it on. The fuse box in the cellar is unknown territory. She makes coffee on the gas stove, eats shrink-wrapped ham and bread and butter, pickled onions from a jar. In the evenings, when the sun peels away from the easternmost parts of the house, she retreats by degrees to the brighter rooms until there is no more daylight, and then she goes to sleep.

She cannot watch television, though this is only a minor irritation as all she ever really watches are the shopping channels and the twenty-four-hour mediums. *Call now for a personal consultation with an experienced psychic in the comfort of your very own home.* Her type of television is the sort that Daniel says speaks to a weakness of character (although admittedly a lot speaks to Daniel of a weakness of character: a fondness for jelly sweets, the refusal to give dogs human names, hair grown past the shoulders, the Tolkien books). He has, in the past, tried to educate her, turning on the History Channel, documentaries about beluga whales. The first time, walking in on Nicola watching QVC in bed, tangle of orange peel in her lap, he had cocked his head to the side and squinted at the screen.

'What's that they're selling?'

'Fabergé eggs.'

'Not real ones?'

'I don't know. If you buy half a dozen, they send you a hutch to keep them in.'

She had an itchy dialling finger, an overzealous eye for a bargain. The weekly thud of pink-wrapped packages in the letter cage had quickly become a source of tension; Daniel stiffly handing over boxes containing pizza scissors, ceramic knife sets, printed scarves, cultured pearls set in abalone.

'What have you bought this time?'

'It's a hand-carved set of wooden fruit. I thought we could display it in the hall.'

'I keep the Japanese maquettes in the hall.'

'I know, but there's space for two things.'

'What's that?'

'I think that's a kiwi. I don't know. They don't look quite how they looked on TV.'

On the beach, a red-haired woman is walking a child along the sand on a pair of elastic reins. The child can be no more than three, jangle-boned, with the shambling, drunken gait of one whose legs have only very recently been introduced to one another. Lashed to the red-haired woman's wrist, he drags towards the headland, where the men with litter-pickers have now paused to inspect their haul. It is low tide, the sea pretending innocence. Squinting down along the line of the shore, Nicola watches the gentle pull of outgoing water, the glassy sink and swallow, waves drawing back like lips revealing teeth.

There is a sudden commotion, the tethered child making a lurch towards something in the sand – a jellyfish, split open and unbodied, a mess of tentacles and bells and polyps that the men running clean-up operations have failed to sweep away. The red-haired woman gives a mighty tug on the reins, enough to haul the child back and halfway off his feet, at which surprise he stumbles over and starts crying. From the deck, Nicola watches as one of the men from the clean-up crew approaches to assess the situation, the red-haired woman already yanking the child up by his wrist and shaking him – the twist of nails in skin. The man holds up his hands, litter-picker swinging jauntily outwards: *what seems to be the problem, ma'am?* The woman turns on him, jabs a finger into his chest, gesturing first to the litter-picker and then to the jellyfish. The child, wrist still grasped in her other hand, staggers back and forth with her gesticulation, snivelling quickly curtailed by fascination at this sudden opening of hostilities. The man drops his hands, drops back. He swings his litter-picker down, planting it in the sand before changing his mind and looping it upwards, tapping it into his palm like a policeman with a truncheon.

The two of them argue, duelling pointed fingers. The crux of the matter seems to be that the red-haired woman holds the clean-up crew responsible for the child nearly stumbling on a jellyfish, while the man holds the woman responsible for not purchasing a shorter set of reins. The woman jabs at his chest twice more, the man parrying each time with the litter-picker. In her head, Nicola constructs bits and pieces of the conversation – argues both cases, for and against. Meanwhile, the child, working his wrist free of his mother's grasp, totters back towards the jellyfish with renewed purpose, as the voices of the adults are lost to an easterly wind.

+

She has been here over a week now and still considers herself to be essentially engaged in a siege situation. The food is not holding up quite as she had imagined: two pints of milk, one already curdled; a bag of oranges, three eaten, six rotted; six tins of tuna, one of sweetcorn; two packets of ham, two of prawns, two salami; a pineapple, impenetrable; the jar of pickled onions; a multipack of crackers; a block of cheese; a bar of chocolate; a loaf of bread turned white with creeping mould.

If she were Cece, she would have brought along pasta or potatoes; food suitable for long internments with only a gas cooker for company. If she were Cece, she would have thought to bring a can-opener too. By the third day, she is roiling with pickled onions, sore-gummed from shards of cracker. The unrefrigerated ham is growing an odd, oyster-coloured film along its rind.

This ignobility of rotted bread and milk is not what she would have hoped, though she can't deny it adds something bohemian to the situation. The house – dust-sheeted, its swimming pool drained – seems oddly suited, in its current state, to meals of Sun-Maid raisins and orange cheese eaten on the floor. In the afternoons before the sun runs out, she sits in the dining room overlooking the steep incline of cliffs, stacking miniature towers of crackers which she then covers with marmalade and eats over several long minutes, pretending entire banquets from her customary place at the table's head.

Daniel has already gutted the place of anything really worth taking. The majority of the furniture sold at auction as long ago as November, and most of the blue and white also seems to have been snaffled up around that time. Faded patches where the paintings used to hang – a common phenomenon for which Nicola was once startled to realise there is no formal name – disfigure every room in the house. An exercise in barefaced deception. Daniel had gone ahead and sold the Persian rugs and a good percentage of the silver even before asking for a divorce.

What remains – somewhat pointedly, in Nicola's opinion – are many of her QVC acquisitions. A shelf of Russian dolls painted to resemble the Muppets. A machine for counting change. A large pottery cat in whose hollow skull umbrellas can be stored. Between the empty spaces left by Daniel's confiscations, her personal effects remain like a series of insults. A lamp shaped like a goldfish bowl, an egg timer filled with indigo sand. These objects sit around the house like a dumping of useless artefacts; archaeological pieces too mundane to be brought back from the dig.

The divorce has been in the works over six months and

Nicola has given up trying to keep track of where things stand. Her finger has mottled up around her wedding ring, a swell towards the knot of the knuckle like the time she ate rock oysters on her fifteenth birthday and had to be taken to A&E. Every morning, before the heat of the day takes her body and makes it sticky and intractable, she grasps the ring and circles it, twisting back and forth in a vain attempt to take her finger by surprise, slip it up and off before the swelling can stop her. It never works – her left hand is too clever for her right.

'Bacon grease,' Cece had said on the telephone (this was some months before Nicola stole Cece's car to drive down to the beach house and summarily surrendered her right to good advice). 'Or soak your fingers in salt water. It pulls the moisture out of the skin.'

'I tried that,' Nicola had replied. 'And grapefruit balm and salt scrub and keeping my hand elevated fifteen hours a day. Nothing works.'

'Well, I don't know, then.' Cece's children in the background barked instructions for a game of Twister – *left hand red!* 'Cut your finger off or just don't get divorced, I suppose. What do I know.'

+

Ball lightning hits the patio doors. Wild blue bounce, like a tumbling of hailstones. She watches the storm from the kitchen windows and wonders whether the buffeted sea will soon expel more bodies. Her telephone psychics would be helpful here. *I'm sensing some sort of invertebrate, a whole lot of them, in fact.*

The night she and Daniel met, there had been a thunderstorm. A feeble happening, in truth, three cracks of lightning and a drop in pressure, though still enough to keep Cece's dinner guests entertained. Cece had not seated them together, more concerned with fixing Daniel up with a friend of hers who sold Mannerist art and owned a pack of shih-tzus named for the phases of the moon. *Gibbous is a little scamp, he keeps Crescent and First Quarter on their toes.*

'My sister's the pretty one,' Cece had announced, by way of introduction when Nicola first arrived. 'Our father called her the precious cargo. So everyone be on your best behaviour.'

She had seated her next to an older man who had lectured her on jurisprudence for the duration of the fish course and then excused himself for the lavatory with an expression which very much suggested that Nicola had been the one boring him. It was at this point that Daniel had slid in beside her, leaving the shih-tzu owner, as Cece would lament some time later, quite humiliated five seats down.

'You looked in need of rescuing,' had been his opening salvo. The sudden vastness of him, dark block against the lightning spill.

'I can take care of myself,' she'd responded, squaring shoulders, though he had only shaken his head.

'Can't leave a lady in danger, as my father used to say.'

He had driven her to the beach house that very night –

three hours of frantic getaway in a vast September dark. She had let him carry her off, very much as a prize from a captured citadel, let him talk in circles about showing her this place he thought would suit her, a refuge from the pressures of the world. Holding her hand to steer her out of the path of some fox mess in the driveway, he had murmured, 'Watch your step,' in a manner both cautionary and imperative. He had kissed her in the hallway, led her out onto the deck.

Of course, divorcing had been different. No thunderstorm, only a spiralling wind.

+

She doesn't sleep well. She tries honey, pulls up lavender from the bushes that straggle through the slats of the deck. Daniel has had the bed removed, yet still she sleeps within its confines, rectangular phantom in the centre of the room. From this pretence of space, she can play-act other nights, other weekends, when the house was furnished with more than the memory of things.

Midnight in a hot September, beat of moths against the overhead lamp. July, slick with sweat, Daniel mixing prairie oysters and complaining about his eyes.

A month after they were first married, they had driven up to the house in a sultry twilight, car lights on the water dimmed to white. Crashing in, stumbling to the bedroom, she had pushed him backwards, bared her teeth like knuckles, accused him of driving drunk.

'Speak for yourself,' he had snorted – the furtive joy of him, grabbing at her hair. 'Orange juice all night. Someone had to be the designated driver if you were going to get all drunk drunk.'

'Drunk drunk,' she had repeated, enjoying the sound of it. The dense forgiveness of his expression, the hard clasp of hands on her waist.

In the morning, she had woken to a drifting of summer rain. Heavy arms around her, tricky to escape. Rolling out, she had considered Daniel, snoring gently, glaring in his sleep, as if in disapproval. She had known him then, seen his werewolf skin beneath the surface. Without waking him, she had left the room and wandered out onto the deck in her dressing gown, bare feet slippery on the slats. Beyond the sand, the water had frothed with animation, as though rising up to meet the rain. The tide had been on the wane, the beach filled with the everyday litter of ascophyllum, cuttle-bones and beer cans. The spider crabs had emerged from their hiding places and made for the relative safety of the flats.

+

There has been no knocking since the third day, when some-one from the offices of Daniel's lawyer had driven down in a Prius and camped outside the house.

'The point is to nip this in the bud,' he had called through the letterbox, fanning fingers through the copper flap like some encroaching insect. 'We can sort this out quickly and quietly. Call it a brief lapse in judgement. It's been an emotional time. Tricky business, difficult decisions. No harm, no foul. Et cetera.'

Sitting at the bottom of the hall stairs, she had nibbled on salami and pictured Daniel's lawyer – his almost uncanny hairlessness, as though he had been dipped in lye. At their last meeting, he had leant over the table towards her and she had watched a bead of sweat travel in a seamless line from his crown to the centre of his lip, where he had halted it with a quickly darting tongue. *Do correct me if I'm wrong, of course, but both my records and my client's testimony state that you have actually never worked, Mrs Carmichael. That you have in fact been dependent on the generosity of others your entire life – is this the case?*

At the letterbox, the fingers had flapped, retracted, the voice behind the door becoming irritable. 'Mrs Carmichael, I don't know you but I can't imagine any sane woman would want to be stuck with an injunction, let alone a charge of trespassing, and that's what's going to happen if you continue this stunt. If you just open the door and talk with me, I'm sure we can sort this out.'

Shrugging a shoulder, Nicola had crossed to the door – barricaded with a scuttle of chairs – and posted the remainder of her salami out through the letterbox before wandering away. (She regrets this gesture now, a little. With the ham on the turn, there is scant protein left amongst her rations.)

Whether or not the threat to return with an injunction was a serious one, there have been no visitors since the first. Of course, there may well have been phone calls but she is thankfully in no position to say. She has, it is true, half-expected Cece to come chasing her, but perhaps her sister's current lack of a car is owed something for that delay.

In the dining room, between marmalade-slathered crackers, she acts out scenes of high drama, imagining scenarios, gesticulating to the blank spaces on the walls.

'What did you think you were achieving?' her sister would say – her narrow limbs, ponytail cuffed in Hermès. 'Daniel takes the beach house in the divorce so you immediately drive down and barricade yourself in? You know my children practise better conflict resolution than you.'

'He doesn't even want it,' Nicola would reply. 'He owned it before we met, he never used it. And yet now he's threatening to sell it. Just because he knows I want it. He's like a child who wrecks a toy he never plays with when his mother tries to give it away.'

'That is ten-pence psychology,' Cece would say. 'You don't know what you're talking about. If anyone's being childish here it's you.'

'You're supposed to be on my side,' Nicola would whine – whines aloud, too, in the dining room, to no one.

+

The jellyfish return again the next day. Flooding the shoreline in the early morning like a littering of plastic, the beach foul-breathed after a stormy night. The summer is becoming unpredictable, rain-swollen – a white, fetid season, filthy with cloud.

From the deck, Nicola watches the commotion. Teenagers with their phones out, filming videos of one another poking jellyfish with sticks. Towards the foreland, an elderly couple are walking arm in arm, in matching jackets. The woman is bent over, great chin and wattle hanging down beyond her breastbone. The man, though tall and relatively sprightly, walks bent over to the same degree, keeping pace with her halting step. As they approach a jellyfish, the man rears upright, just long enough to scout a clear path around the obstacle, before dropping back into his imitation hunch and towing the woman safely up the bay.

Throughout the morning, Nicola watches for the red-headed woman and her tethered child, although neither one appears. Around noon, a television crew arrives to shoot a brief piece – the hosts of a general-interest show Nicola half-remembers Daniel watching, talking genially to each other with their shoes encased in plastic bags. *'Potential tourist attraction, yes – but is this plague symptomatic of something more serious, Cathy?'* – *'Actually, Tim, I think you'll find that "plague" is a word usually only applied to insects.'*

Behind them, the teenagers dance about for the cameras, sticking out their tongues and waving until the director has to pause filming to ask them to settle down.

In the afternoon, she sits in the living room and tries to ignore her growling stomach. She is approaching emergency levels with her rations but the prospect of leaving the house to search for food seems only to invite invasion. If she were Cece, she would have brought a cooler. If she were Cece, she would have thought this through.

She sets up the plastic chess set and plays herself with a jumbled, Ludo-like approach to the rules, jumping bishops over knights and moving queens with abandon. Early on, Daniel had showed her a photograph of himself at a junior school chess tournament – ten years old, top-heavy with braces and a nose to grow into, sourly clutching a participation prize.

'I hadn't cracked the code yet,' he had said, laying the chess set out between them, and she had loved him for his straight teeth and strident nose and the fact that he couldn't bear to lose at anything. He had taught her chess strategies and combinations, smacking her hands away from impulse moves.

'There are safer ways to get there,' he would say, time and time again, repositioning her pawns around the king. 'You don't have to be silly about it. There's never any need to lose, if you only use your head.'

+

Daniel's lawyer has a voice like unguent. As he speaks through the letterbox, she imagines him licking up sweat with the moist dark dab of his tongue.

'Mrs Carmichael, I have here written instruction for you to vacate the premises no later than tomorrow afternoon. We're not playing games here, girlie. This is legal imbroglio. You have to think about where you stand.'

He posts the papers and retreats, though regrettably she has now run out of salami to post back out. Picking up the collection of envelopes, she moves immediately to one addressed in Daniel's handwriting, though the note inside is only a typed rehashing of all the offers he has made her over the past six months: the Alfa Romeo, a sterling-silver knife set, a collection of Danish miniatures, half the books, half the frequent-flier miles, all the jewellery free and clear.

'My heart bleeds,' Cece had said, looking over a similar list only weeks after the divorce was first floated. Slicing blue cheese. Smear of apricot jam at her lip. 'He takes the car so you only get the other car. He takes the credit cards so you only get the gold bullion and the diamond mine.'

She takes the envelopes through to the kitchen and wanders out onto the deck. For the fourth or fifth time, the jellyfish have flooded the shore, but this time the men from the clean-up crew have hit upon the idea of building a bonfire. Not far from the headland, a great tower of bodies is forming – headless, shapeless things stacked one and another, the flimsy outlines of creatures drained of all substance, souping down into the bedrock of the shore. The television crew has returned and is filming a walk-and-talk along the ridge of the dunes. '*And what I believe we can expect in a matter of minutes, Cathy, is an inflagration potentially unlike any we have seen before.*' – '*A conflagration, Tim. Inflagration isn't a word.*'

Nicola watches the small crowd milling around the bonfire, men heaving shovelfuls onto the pile. The fire, when it goes up, is a faint and queasy blue, filling the air with the smell of something boiling. On the deck, Nicola folds in half the typed page she is still holding and finds a further scribble in black biro overleaf.

Nicola for God's sake, grow up

She is out of food, except for crackers, which have grown soft from being left unwrapped. With nothing to occupy her, she falls asleep on the floor of the bedroom in the early afternoon. She dreams first about her wedding: the prawn cocktails in martini glasses and Daniel swinging her around to 'Try a Little Tenderness'. Cece had given a speech about her little sister – *We always knew Nic would find someone dependable* – and Nicola had tried to make her own toast, although at this point, the dream changes and she imagines herself a jellyfish – a blind thing, tearable as paper, sinking down beneath black water on a moonless febrile night.

+

Before their father died, he had called her the princess, the precious cargo. Pressed his hands together and mimed an attendant's bow.

'There is a lack of self-preservation about you,' Cece had said, midway through their father's funeral, 'which is frankly a vanity. You assume other people will care enough to look after you.'

In asking for a divorce, Daniel had told her he knew that it was at least partially his fault. Leaning over with his hands on his knees, he had spoken to the floor of the deck, explaining that he hadn't considered the pitfalls inherent in really taking ownership of someone. She had told him, as she had that first night at dinner, that she could actually take care of herself, though he had only shaken his head once again and taken his ring off, easy as pie.

+

In the evening, Nicola leaves the house and walks down the narrow jag of path onto the beach. The bonfire has burned itself out over the course of the day and what is left is only skeletal. A coil of indigo smoke. The shore is quiet, clean, the way it had been when Daniel first walked her down it, holding her hand and her elbow to guide her over divots in the sand. She navigates her own way now, turns her ankle only briefly on the slope.

Up over the dunes, she can see the deck that wraps around the house, the plates and cups she has left there, the dressing gown she has abandoned to the back of a chair. Daniel's lawyer will not, she imagines, appreciate the mess when he returns tomorrow, nor will he appreciate the empty house or the fact that she has left the front door open, thrown the windows wide on both the north and southern sides, left the key under the mat.

The evening is soft now, wheel of night gulls on the water. In her bag, she has the Russian dolls from QVC, the egg timer filled with coloured sand, the machine for counting change. The pottery cat she has had to leave behind, being too unwieldy to lift.

It is just after ten in the evening, no particular rush to be gone. She sits down in the sand, a spot just beyond the wrack line, and works idly at the ring on her still-swollen finger, turning it round in fruitless circles, never raising it above the knuckle. There will be more jellyfish. Later, washing up in the tight apple-light that follows dawn, a product of the early tide. When they come, she will still be here, salt-rimed from a night on the shore. She will lay herself down, await the convocation. Jellyfish beaching against her arms and legs, the crest of body on delicate body. They will cover her, glove her hands, circle her ankles. Dependant on species, it can take a jellyfish up to fifty minutes to die once out of water. In the thin lifeline of a waning tide, that time can be easily tripled. Nicola will stay with them well into the morning, their pulsing bells like so many painful hearts. Blanketed, almost head to toe, she will feel the tide recede. Her fingers will come to feel a touch gelatinous at their points, softened along their webbing. She will imagine herself sinking down, becoming something less than solid, spilling insides onto the sand.

Cassandra After

The fact of my girlfriend's return was incontestable. She sat on my sofa and dripped water onto the rug. My mother had always told me it was better not to answer the door between midnight and three a.m. *Strange neighbourhood,* she would say, sounding more paranoid than she meant to, *buy a deadbolt, keep your curtains shut.*

It is a Jewish custom to cover mirrors with cloth after a death but I was Catholic by birth and agnostic by trickledown and checked my reflection compulsively before answering doors. The night my girlfriend knocked, my face in the glass was like newsprint, inky around the eyes and under the collar. She stood there on the doorstep in the clothes in which she'd been buried, chucked me under the chin the way she used to do and told me I looked like I hadn't been sleeping. *Bad for the skin, darling girl. Stop drinking coffee.* She had been dead six months and her skin was coming away from the bone, although she seemed not to notice this.

The Catholic Church traditionally designates three stages of mourning – heavy, half and light. My girlfriend had once joked that this sounded like the branding on sanitary towels. *Half mourning, for your three-day flow.* Well into the nineteen-fifties, Catholic widows had been expected to observe a year of heavy mourning, followed by six months each of half and light mourning, during which they could only wear clothes in black and white mixtures, soft greys and occasional mauves. I read this in a book on funeral etiquette I had borrowed from the library, noting also a caveat in 'Spousal Grief Procedure' that provision could be made to lessen the mourning period if the widow found someone she considered a viable suitor after the passing of a year. I had held on to the book some months past its return date and had started receiving irate messages from the library by the time my girlfriend came back.

The issue, of course, was that she had been buried and now she wasn't, although this could be said to be the case for a lot of things. I had once been a practising Catholic and now I wasn't. Not unlike my religious conviction, her death had simply lapsed. I let her in and left her sitting on the sofa while I microwaved some Chinese rice and poured pineapple juice into a glass. It was her comfort meal – grease and bromelain. She had often lectured me on pineapple's anti-inflammatory properties, how it helped prevent cataracts and heart disease. Taking the rice out of the microwave, I noticed I had scribbled the word *teeth* on my hand to remind myself to brush them. Since my girlfriend's death, I had developed the habit of going to bed unwashed and waking up with my tongue furred over and tasting strangely of iodine.

She raised an eyebrow when I handed her the food, although she ate obligingly and only seemed a little abashed when a mouthful lodged in her throat and had to be coughed back up. *No digestion*, she said, by way of explanation, *sweet of you though.* I sat on the coffee table and faced her, taking in the mud on her sleeves. I registered a distant sort of alarm, a feeling which arose like obligation, like the pressure to clap at the end of a performance, regardless of its merit. Fear sat only gently at the base of my spine, waiting for a reason to climb a little further. She wriggled a shoulder at me – *see something you like?* – and the exposed tendons around her collarbone squeezed and released.

+

Once, at a book launch, I leant up against a table stacked with queer literature and knocked a plastic glass of wine to the floor. *Steady on*, she said, a stranger then – faux-leather trousers, emblematic of a perfect self-possession. She perched on the opposite end of the table and nudged a toe into the spreading pool of wine. *Do you know the author*, she asked, nodding towards the crowd now formed around the woman signing copies, *or do you just like to make scenes in bookshops?* She was taller than me, swimming cap of blonde hair. I was wearing a trouser suit – not my usual look, just something I was trying – and I often wondered afterwards whether she would have spoken to me if I'd been dressed differently.

She told me her name was Cassandra and pulled a looning, prophetess expression, which made me laugh. She scribbled her number inside her copy of the book being launched and handed it to me. When I opened it up later, I noticed that she had already had the copy signed, her number inked beneath the author's scrawl of *Cassie, I could never have done this without you.*

+

After failing to finish the rice I had given her, Cassandra sat back against the sofa cushions and asked when I'd last cut my hair. She held her glass of juice a little slackly and I felt nervous that she might decide to pour it on the carpet or throw it in my face. Sitting low against the blanket my mother had crocheted to cover the boot marks on my second-hand sofa, she was a gentle sort of horror; the look of a girl removed from a coffin by a lunatic and placed upright to partake in a dinner party.

She told me idly that she had found a bunch of flowers against her headstone with a label reading *RIP Clive* and that she had spent the best part of an hour wandering the cemetery looking for the correct place to put it. *There weren't any Clives anywhere near me*, she explained, *but it felt churlish not to look.* She had eventually ended up leaving the bouquet at the graveside of someone named Trevor, a name which she claimed to be close enough to Clive in era and sociological type as to be tantamount to the same thing. *What I mean to say by all this is that I'm sorry it took me so long to get here,* she added, setting her juice down on the coffee table and moving a hand to my leg. Her fingernails, I noted, were filthy, her expression odd, and my body felt tight as a fist, chilly tension seizing up the muscles in my legs.

Traditional Catholic funeral custom strongly favours burial over the ritual of cremation. This is mostly to do with the belief in the resurrection of the body, an oddly terms-and-conditions approach to the holy mysteries which dictates that only those buried intact will be granted eternal life. The thought has always reminded me of a Sunday school gag – my cousins smoking cigarettes under the vestibule window, flicking ash onto the toes of my shoes and getting me to kick upwards: *And on the third day he rose again! Oh no, wait, he was cremated. False alarm.* My girlfriend was not a Catholic but chose to be buried anyway, a decision she had communicated to me in a highly considered fashion one day whilst refusing to explain her logic or why she had brought it up. I told her that I wanted to be cremated, although this was more of a snipe at the fact that I happened to be chilly that day. She took my hands and blew on them and I felt unaccountably irritated, pulling one hand away and wiping it when she blew too hard and left little flecks of spit on my fingertips. *There's a selfishness to you,* she said, perhaps in response to this or perhaps to something other. *A mean streak. You're not always very kind to people.* I objected to this and took her judgement away to stew over, finally coming to the conclusion that she was right after all and enjoying that, in a childish, contrary way. It became oddly like permission, this acknowledgement – the mean streak, once spoken aloud, a quality I found too easy to excuse in myself.

+

She had told me that the women in her family tended to die oddly, writing a list on the back of a canteen serviette after finishing a slice of opera cake. It was an oddly sexy move, flipping the napkin before she slid it over to me, like an offer in a silent auction. I flipped it back and read it while she asked for the bill, taking note of the tall, bent consonants that seemed to smuggle vowels across the paper.

- Great-Aunt Helen, died in the surf at Margate, blanketed with jellyfish
- Grandma Louise, tried to kill herself first by eating a pot of poinsettias (which didn't work) and then by swallowing bleach (which did)
- Third Cousin Caroline, fell from a fourth-storey window taking delivery of a Christmas tree

The list ran to some twelve or thirteen bullets and devolved from close kin to the merely tangential. Second Cousin Anya (some five times removed) was documented to have been impaled on the antlers of a stag, whilst Marina (relation unspecified – something to do with her great-grandma's third husband) was rather cryptically billed as having become convinced of a terrible thirst. She paid the bill while I was reading and waved a hand at my protestation. *Stands to reason I won't be around as long as you*, she said, tapping her finger against the napkin, *might as well throw my money around.*

This trip to the canteen was our third date, although only on a kind of technicality. The first date (so-called) comprised the encounter in the bookshop. The second was prompted by a panicked late-night phone call, which I had instigated after convincing myself I wasn't going to and she suggested a drink. I dressed quickly after ending that call, throwing on a dark red jumper which I hoped might distract her attention from the scab I had picked at my chin. She found me outside the pub she had suggested, fifteen minutes after we were due to meet, saying cheerfully that she had been around the whole place twice and hadn't recognised me at all. The date was a curious mix of natural and stilted, Cassandra asking once if I had somewhere else to be but only smiling when I queried this. *Chill out. You're wriggling around all over the place.*

+

There was a place in the side of her cheek where the skin had come away enough to reveal the upward slant of her teeth. I stared at it as she talked, thinking of the cutaway drawings in biology textbooks, the human body half revealed like a dollhouse, layers of dermis and fatty tissue drawn back to show an annotated cross-section of liver and lungs. I took away the unfinished bowl of rice and the juice glass and set them on the kitchen counter, squinting as I did so at the postcard she had once tacked to my fridge. A cartoon print of a city, underscored by thick black print: *There may be no heaven anywhere but somewhere there is a San Francisco.* I had taken this postcard down and put it up again several times in the weeks after she died, pacing the kitchen with it held between thumb and forefinger, approaching the bin but never moving to throw it away. I had done all kinds of things in those tight, toothsome weeks which had latched themselves to my body like fangs embedded in flesh. I'd burned smudge sticks and thrown open the windows, hoping birds would fly into the house. I'd called up radio stations and taken part in competitions to win Toyotas and kitchen blenders and holidays to Spain. One morning, possessed of a strange mania, I had pulled two fingernails out at the root and afterwards had stood looking at them for several minutes before wrapping them, dropping them in the toilet and flushing them away.

Where's all your fruit, Cassandra said, having meanwhile shifted from the sofa and moved to join me by the fridge. She was wet, a clammy waterlogged permanence, and her hair dripped silt onto the kitchen tiles. She was looking over at my fruit bowl, which I had allowed to grow delinquent and furry with ancient pomegranates. I told her I couldn't remember the last time I'd been shopping and she rolled her eyes at me. *I've always thought it's a miracle you don't get scurvy.* I thought about all the other things I had ceased to do reliably – the electric bills I'd put through the shredder, the dwarf irises I had allowed to die in their planters. She told me she would pop to the corner shop when it got a little lighter and buy me a bag of blood oranges but I told her she might scare the other customers. *Well I wouldn't want to embarrass you*, she said coolly in response to this. I found I suddenly doubted the strength in my upper body, a sensation of air leaking from tyres slashed by glass. The fear that had settled at the small of my back crept a little higher, clutching like unfriendly hands.

Beyond the kitchen window, the sky was the colour of whaleskin. It occurred to me that I was sweating, although the night was chilly, my legs smudged green with bruises from all the times I had slammed them into doors and the sides of coffee tables, wandering the house in a daze. *So anyway*, Cassandra said, as if resuming a perfectly normal conversation, *tell me everything. I want to know what you've been up to.* I looked at her and thought about how I had always loved her attention and simultaneously hated too much of it. She met my gaze with equanimity, the split in her lip like a lightning-burst strip of fence. *Nothing much*, I said, after a pause, *getting on with things. I'm more interested to know what's been going on with you.*

She shook her head. *You never want to talk about you. I know you think it's being polite but actually it just makes me feel like you don't trust me.* I sighed, trying to balance the logic of her language against the insanity of her appearance in my kitchen. She shook her head again and a segment of earthworm dropped out of her ear.

+

She had taken me to galleries and Ukrainian cafés and the unfamiliar sections of bookshops. Afternoon dates, lemon-skied and out in the open – I had held her hand on the overground and let her kiss me over rugelach. *Look at your hair*, she had often said, *look at your hands, look at the way you say things.* It was her way of complimenting me, though it also doubled as a kind of homework, to be held up to such scrutiny. For my birthday, two months after we'd first met, she took me for Muscadet and oysters at a place she knew in the city and we both managed to get ludicrously drunk in the space of about an hour. The oysters were good, cheaply decadent; pucker-salt and bone and tide. I watched her throat moving as she swallowed and thought of all the boys I had ever kissed at school. *What d'you think?* she asked, licking her bottom lip and then the points of her incisors. I told her about how my father had always liked to pinch lemon over oysters, the quailing shrink of the creamy little creatures from the sting. *I didn't realise you'd had them before,* she'd replied, swinging back on her barstool as though pushed. *There's me thinking I'm broadening your horizons!* I laughed at this, refilled her wine glass and threw back an oyster with uncharacteristic elan. *You're so patronising. Pass me another.*

In the evenings after our dates, I took to smearing my hands with lotion to force myself to wait before replying to her messages. *Had a gorgeous time*, she would text me, then a picture of a dog she had seen on a train. I would wait until my hands dried, cycling as I did through impatience, through apathy, through the surprising and fleeting desire to never text her again. *Me too*, I would always reply, shortly after getting over this last impulse and starting the cycle anew. Then

I would tell her what music I was listening to and she would give me her opinions and we would go on that way until one of us fell asleep.

So you're a lesbian now, a friend had asked me, over tea and boxed doughnuts. I had tried to explain my thoughts on the Kinsey scale, to explain that it wasn't that exactly but it wasn't bisexuality either, and had given up halfway through.

One night, Cassandra and I had gone out together to a mostly male gay club in the city. It was almost autumn, chilly weather scraping like nails down a board, and she threw her jacket over my shoulders in the queue. I kissed her in response to this and immediately wished I hadn't, for a group of men on the kerb cheered us and I pulled away embarrassed and turned my ankle off the edge of my shoe. Inside, I bought us drinks and tried to avoid being kissed again, though she caught me on the cheek and then on the corner of my lip. On the dancefloor, she slung her bare arms around my shoulders and gave me such a violent electric shock that I staggered away from her. We ended up dancing with a group of largely indifferent men, the friendliest of whom tugged my ponytail and shouted, apropos of nothing much, *I love a trier.* I sank suddenly, doused by tequila and loud music, danced ridiculously and wrapped my arms around my girlfriend's neck. *It's so cheesy!* I apparently screamed at her at one point and she petted my face and told me not to offend the clientele.

When we left the club, I found that someone had stolen my wallet and I ended the evening crying messily in an all-night café. Sitting slanted at a table by the window, I scrambled repeatedly through my handbag, lash-stuck and salty with the start of dry heaves. Cassandra slotted sharply into my vision, squatting down with her hands on my thighs. I remember little of what was actually said that night, but I know I told her this felt like a punishment and I know she rolled her eyes. *It can't always be about shame*, she said, gesturing around her in a way I knew was meant to encompass more than just the café; the whole night, everything.

The next day, I woke up hungover and went to the Catholic church at the end of my road, a place I had never once been. The place smelled, not of incense, as Catholic churches do in memoirs, but of sweat and furniture polish, stale bread and Gucci Guilty. Someone at the door handed me a hymnal – finger marks on sticky-back plastic. I sat in a pew near the back and leafed through the index, trying to decipher the Sunday school graffiti: *Roxane was here; one holy catholic and APOSTOLIC church; saint cecilia was a lezzer & so was saint louise.*

Afterwards, Cassandra came to find me, bearing coffee and apple turnovers and offering to help me order a new bank card and a new driving licence. She slid an arm around me and kissed me on the side of mouth in a way that made me love her terribly, though I had promised God the opposite only minutes before.

+

You could tell the library book on mourning customs was dated, primarily because of the emphasis it placed on the bereaved abstaining from balls and galas in the months after a death.

One is advised, it read, *to refrain from public functions during the mourning period, as well as private parties and large events hosted in the home. One may dine with select friends and continue such sports and pastimes as might be considered reasonably appropriate, but costume should be dark-coloured and suited only to the sport at hand.*

A *widow,* it continued, *should accept no overt or clandestine romantic attentions for the space of one year. If this rule is disregarded, all mourning attire and pretence of adherence to the mourning period should be entirely dropped.*

In the kitchen, Cassandra had turned on the radio and was singing along to the song by Barry Manilow about waving goodbye and being back in a city where nothing seemed clear. In the overhead light, I could see how thin her hair was and the way her teeth rattled oddly in their sockets, displaced by so much dirt and so much time spent out of sight. *Is this a haunting?* I asked her and she looked at me as if surprised. *No,* she said, turning the radio down, *not technically. More like a manifestation.* I accused her of quibbling over semantics and she accused me of being incapable of nuance. We argued and it all felt very much the way it used to, except for the way her bones showed through her skin.

Is 'haunted' something you feel, particularly? she queried, and I looked at her quickly. Her expression was even but there was something pointed and rather bitter about the air-starved cast of her gaze. *I mean in general*, she prodded, though I refused to take the bait.

You look tired, she said at length and reached out to push my hair away from my face, although her fingers were clammy and made my forehead feel clammy too. *I don't think*, I wanted to say, *that I ever deserved your attention*, though I only shrugged and turned away from her, trying to remember how people banished ghosts in films. On the kitchen countertop, I noted that my phone was flashing – green light, rather than blue, which meant it was a message from someone on a dating website.

New here, my profile said, *not sure what I'm looking for*.

+

The weekend after I'd first slept with my girlfriend, I went to get a haircut. My hairdresser, a woman prone to overshare, told me unprompted that a female friend of hers had recently 'gone gay' and that she, my hairdresser, wasn't sure she still wanted to invite her to a standing dinner they held every second Sunday of the month. The sensation was not unlike the slip of missing a step, or the realisation that someone you are having an emotional moment with is much drunker than you'd thought they were. She continued to cut my hair and I remained in my seat and did not ask her to explain what she meant exactly. After she finished, I removed the black smock she had velcroed around me and my hair fell like something tipped from a jar.

Cassandra was a good kisser, a good talker, a good judge of

pace. I was bad at sex and knew it, though I had always been bad at it and stressed that this was not about her. I explained to her the way I felt I floated up out of myself and observed the whole thing loosely, from a distance. I explained the way I felt no better or worse after doing it, only an overwhelming sense of having missed the point. She shook her head at this and kissed me and told me I was taking things far too seriously. Later on, we fell asleep together and I woke up gasping from a nightmare that she was sinking claws into my sides.

I had a bad body around that time – creaking joints and difficult digestion, a martyr to mouth ulcers and bleeding gums. My turn-ons included being bitten and being grabbed by the roots of my hair. During sex, my girlfriend sometimes told me she had never wanted anyone more and I sometimes told her the same thing and sometimes didn't say anything at all. After sex, she liked to eat individual rice puddings which she kept in the fridge at my house. On Saturday mornings, she would go swimming in the lake near the common whilst I did my laundry and vacuumed the house. She would come back smelling of moss and duckweed and I would towel her hair and read her horoscope from the back pages of the paper. On Sundays, we would stay in, just us, watch movies together and make up pasta sauces, and those were often my favourite times.

It's kind of a holiday though, isn't it, a friend asked me, licking jam and doughnut sugar from the knuckle of one thumb. *The girl thing. Only a temporary solution.* I thought about Cassandra's list on the back of the napkin, the tacitly promised respite – *Great-Aunt Helen, died in the surf* – and did not know what to say. Occasionally, I convinced myself I had made it all up – love, attraction, all of it – that I had made it up with everyone I'd ever met.

+

I was worried that the sun would start coming up and that she would still be there. I wanted to know whether the mourning book had any etiquette notes on visitations from the recently deceased but it seemed insensitive to check it in front of her. For all her insistence that her presence didn't constitute a haunting, there seemed a strange intent behind her aimlessness, an inability to say something pressing that put me stupidly in mind of movies about ghosts with unfinished business – poltergeists who plagued stately homes in lieu of stating grievances aloud. She circled my kitchen several times, picking things up and dropping them, rearranging the magnets on the fridge. I found myself wishing she'd come back as a vampire or a werewolf, something with fangs and a destructive will. As it was, the onus seemed to be on me to make something of the visit.

I noticed that her body appeared to be holding up poorly. She leant up against the kitchen counter and her knee bent too far backwards – slink of tendons through fragile skin. The flesh around her fingers looked looser than it had an hour ago, the empty nail beds puckered grey. Occasionally, in the old days, I had looked into her ears when she was sleeping and wondered whether her soul might be visible, buried somewhere beneath her cochlea or the soft base of her eardrum. It was strange, now, to be able to look right through her in places – the deep places in her throat and ribcage where the skin had worn away to reveal her dark interiors, the opened hollows of her chest. I had always imagined her soul like a stitch in fabric, metallic thread in wool. Looking into her, I wondered where I could expect to find such a stitch or whether, like so much of what I recognised, it had simply come away from her body and been lost.

What are you thinking, she asked me, and I found I couldn't tell her that I'd missed her, though I had and also wished she'd go away. *It's terrible, when you won't speak to me*, she pressed, and I felt the bitterness, again, around the spaces in the conversation I refused to fill. *It **was** terrible*, she corrected herself, which felt to me like a cheap shot.

+

I had kissed a man, just once at a work event, and afterwards expected Cassandra to be understanding. I'm not sure why I thought this would be the case, really, except to say that I had never been with a woman before and had perhaps naively anticipated the same unconditional support I received from female friends. It didn't mean anything. She cried when I told her and I was unconscionably irritated by it, demanding several times that she listen to me because she wasn't hearing what it was I was trying to say. *What I hear is that you consider us experimentation*, she told me, *that the norm for you is something else.*

163

I didn't know what to say to this and found myself apologising out of sheer surprise at how suddenly I understood my own guilt. *You have a mean streak,* I thought in compulsive, mantra-like circles – a mental voice that was sometimes mine and often Cassandra's. We didn't speak for three days, during which time I became so panicked at the thought of losing her that I sent her a total of thirty-nine hysterically casual messages – a photograph of my breakfast, a quote from a movie, a long text about which of my trains had been delayed that day.

Eventually, I lost all semblance of reason and went round to her house on a Thursday night to apologise, bringing with me a collection of offerings: a bunch of sunflowers and a pack of individual rice puddings. I told her I would try harder and that she should trust me because of that man in the gay club who had identified me as a trier in front of everyone there. *I don't think that was really what he meant,* she replied, but I had amused her enough to let me in and, shortly afterwards, to let me kiss her on the blue recliner she kept in a pool of light beneath a standard lamp. *I feel so much more myself,* I told her, not quite knowing whether I meant at that very moment or more generally since the two of us had met. I ended up staying the night and all of Friday and enjoyed, in that time, a sense of something more decided or more certain, though in truth, had things turned out differently, I cannot say that I wouldn't in time have gone on to ruin things again.

On the Saturday morning, she kissed me and slid out of

bed to go swimming, as she usually did, and did not return. She had no identification on her beyond the address scrawled into the side of her wetsuit, and police might never have known to tell me had I not still been in her bedroom when they knocked.

+

Catholic funerals are often preceded by an evening vigil known as the Reception of the Body. This is an event largely centred around close family – a brief service the night before the funeral, during which the coffin is taken into the church and those closest to the deceased are invited to gather together and pray the rosary. It is intended as a period of quiet and reflection but also allows family first sight of the coffin, in order to lessen the shock on the following day.

My girlfriend, as I've said, wasn't Catholic, and even if she had been, no one knew who I was to invite me to such a vigil, if there had been one to attend.

+

My phone continued to flash green, although my girlfriend appeared not to notice. She was coming apart at the sides by this point, visible through the eaten-up places in her clothes, an awkward unclasping of ribs that seemed to cause her no pain though it stung my shoulders and chest to look at it. I felt a sensation of panic, as though prompted by a timer, a tingle of frustrated tears. I knew a better version of the ghost story taking place in my kitchen would involve my apologising to her for attending her funeral as her neighbour, for not introducing myself to her family and for informing my own parents that I couldn't see them that weekend because a colleague had died. I knew another, more satisfying ghost story would end with revenge wreaked and a filmic wind sweeping my girlfriend's ashes away.

As it was, I spoke badly, stumbled against her baleful expression. I told her I was sorry for not being better or for not trying harder and she looked at me with eyes that were a haunting all their own, whatever she might have said to the contrary. I told her I had rested on the comfortable truth of my limits and she nodded her head in a way that felt cruel and palliative all at once. I pressed my face to her chest in the too-soft place where the skin was still intact and felt I understood the way the surface of the world is thinner in certain places. That these places are where the strange, true things escape.

We didn't talk much more, though she laughed when I said something flippant about not having anything for her to sleep in. In the morning, I told the woman messaging me on the dating site that I couldn't talk to her just yet; I was sweeping the bones of a girl I had loved off the kitchen floor.

salt slow

They find the lobsters in white water. Bobbing belly-up, claws thrown out, like a strewing of tulips. That they float is unsurprising. The salt is heavy here – dead sea, its bodies buoyant. In the thin morning, the lobster shells gleam a slick vermilion, spreading southwards like a bleeding on the tide.

It is a Wednesday, or what they choose to call a Wednesday. In truth, they have long since lost track. The numbering of days has been gradually sacrificed to more pressing concerns; the counting up of cans and bottles, the maintenance of nets, the catching and drying out of fish and strange crustaceans. Time, in its clearest sense, has been abandoned somewhere in the long sleeps and the hourless drifting. Months are all alike on the water, seasons marked by little but the clarity of the light. They label their days as they find them, names to correspond with the poem his mother used to recite to new parents on the obstetrics ward – *Monday's child is fair of face, Tuesday's child is full of grace*. Days of hard squalls and difficult rowing they call Saturdays, days of sunnier aspect they designate Mondays. Thursdays occur only when the horizon seems so distant as to be impossible. There are very few Sundays.

The day they find the lobsters is a bitter one, curling up at its edges like the pages of a book dropped and hastily retrieved from water. He is faint with hunger, ulcers on his tongue, and the ravenous panic with which he leans over the side to grab at the floating bounty is to her a kind of relief. For the last few days he has been listless, dark weight in the stern, and she has found herself growing increasingly uncomfortable. They try their best to ration, bottling anchovies and drying strips of cod to store in papery stacks beneath the seating slats, but their stores are meagre, their little boat a constant rattle of empty space. He has always been quiet, was never voluble even on land, but the vast silence of his hunger is a different thing – stoppered and involuntary, as though his mouth has grown a skin. She has seen him on occasion, hunkered at the gunwale, chewing reflexively on the collar of his jersey. She can look at him in lean times and see nothing at all but teeth.

The lobsters are dead, of course, just like everything that floats on the surface of these waters. They have come across this countless times; the schools of black seabass and bobbing jellyfish, the upturned rafts and coracles that they pillage for remains. *I wonder what killed them*, she will muse, and he will shrug a shoulder. *Who cares.* It was like this when they found the eels, the criss-cross mile upon mile of them, knotted nightmare like a glistening web. He had dismissed the sheer insanity of the scene – the plaited heads and bodies – and simply reached out to disentangle them with the flat blade of an oar.

What's the name for a group of lobsters, he asks now, dumping an armload at her feet. *You know, like a school or a smack.* His sleeves are soaking to the elbows, fingertips already splitting from the salt. She tells him it's a *risk* and he laughs his usual brief laugh, takes up his apple knife and slits a lobster from tail to sternum.

+

A long, wailing motion across the sky. The birds are growing larger.

They drift through fields of dead coral, knocking against husks of petrified crabs, their white meat eaten away. They don't talk much about the shape of her, the way she has to wear his jumper now as her own no longer fits over her belly. It has been some time since the issue became obvious to both of them, the long sickness followed by the hard weight at her hips, but without a reliable means of counting the days, they can only watch and wait. She is no longer seasick, although the motion of the boat gives her bad dreams – thoughts of the ocean overspilling the sides of their craft and getting into bed with her, damp fingers against the small of her back.

He tends to fall quiet again after they find food, although it is a different kind of quiet, a digesting calm that doesn't bother her as much. Sated, his pupils take on the blown-out look she recognises from when they were newly in love and this heartens her, in an odd way, though she knows it has nothing to do with her. She occupies herself as best she can, sands the base of the boat where it is growing sticky, patches small sections of net. They repair and rebuild as required – like Argonauts, piece by piece and always in motion, an ongoing act of damage limitation with nowhere to stop and make berth. Only once, so far, has the boat sprung a leak, and when it did they worked without speaking, she shovelling water with an empty storage jar whilst he patched the hole with the last of the silicone caulk. Afterwards, he had leant back in the stern and covered his face for several minutes, breathing like the sound of something rising through packed earth. She had shifted awkwardly along the edge of the boat to sit beside him. It can be hard, sometimes, for them to come together, the boat's nervous balance easily upset without one of them each at bow and stern to keep it even. Moving is an act of faith, eyebrows furrowed deep. They cross the centre and hope things won't upend.

The birds are gulls and guillemots and frigatebirds; reeling and heavy-chested, the awkward cramp-necked camber of creatures grown out of their natural frames. They are oversized, bloated to albatross proportions, wings like the canvas-backed windcheaters she remembers from days on the beach. Across the tall white scaffolding of sky, they stagger like drunks, unused to their own dimensions. They have grown, she suspects, to make up for the suddenness of water and the sink-down disappearance of safe places to land.

There is almost nowhere, these days, for a flying thing to come down, little but the brief outcrops of sunken headland and the abandoned crafts on which cormorants throng like massing insects, piebald and slick as pitch. Bigger wings, she knows, are a necessity over the ocean as it is now. Bigger wings make it easier to stay airborne for weeks at a time. She watches with nervous eyes when they appear, tallies up different species with a notch of chalk along the baseboards and tries, with a flattened palm held up to the horizon, to keep track of how much larger each bird is than the last.

He talks mumblingly about fashioning a kind of butterfly net, catching and eating a seagull with a salted seaweed crust. She ignores him for the most part, packs her cheeks with lobster roe.

+

When they first met, he had fixed her a Dark and Stormy and told her there was no charge. She had frowned at him, used to the condescending flirtations of bartenders – hollow winks thrown just north of her shoulder. She had pressed her debit card on him, eager to avoid the embarrassment of taking a joke literally, and he had raised an eyebrow in response. *I said no charge.* Shouting over the music. *I'm hitting on you.* Blue eyes, a deep drenched colour. Even before the boat, he had smelled like the sea.

The bar will be underwater now, of course. The university towns drowned quickly – porous stone, too much paper. The night he had stood her a drink it had been raining, though not

the hard, drumming rain that came later (salt rain, sky-wide).
She had abandoned her friends to sit perched all night on a
bar stool, bare legs painful on the vinyl, and he had invented
cocktails for her; whisky blends with ginger beer and star
anise and lemons, glasses cinnamon-rimmed and stuck with
orange rind, spills of vanilla essence and Coca-Cola and Earl
Grey tea. Sticky-drunk, she had stretched her arms across the
surface of the bar, palms up, and showed him the places
where, as a small child, she had burned herself sticking her
hands into an oven to snatch at her mother's coffee cake.
Impatient, she had said and he had licked her wrist and
shaken tequila salt over it.

Later on, she had watched him wipe down the bar with a
dishcloth, the sudden tawdriness of things in closing-time
light. Sweeping peanut shells into a large plastic container,
he had asked her to come home with him, leaning forward to
pluck a highball glass from her hands.

+

It can be strange, on occasion, to remember that they are not
the only ones left. Easier, in some ways, to picture themselves entirely alone – owl and pussycat – and with no hope
of rescue. In truth, there have often been boats; slim horizon
shapes, usually rowing boats or dinghies, though occasionally
they will spot a speedboat, outboard motor cut to bits. Only
once have they come across a yacht, listing hard to starboard
and eerily deserted, ghost ship surrounded by a shivering
cloud of octopuses, clogging the transom and dragging

themselves aboard with enterprising tentacles. *They taste with their skin,* she had said as they slunk up alongside, watching the liquid squeeze of one octopus as it felt its way up over the bowsprit, *I read that somewhere.*

As a general rule, they do not approach strangers. The few obviously peopled crafts they have spotted appear instinctively to keep a distance and they follow this etiquette. They are not altogether sure why they maintain such caution, except to say that the few fellow sailors they have encountered at close quarters have been those they have come across upturned from their vessels and bloated with seawater, boats plundered for their stores by other passing ships. She has turned bandit once or twice herself, although only after checking that whatever poor unfortunate soul they have come across is beyond help.

A small fishing skiff, painted purple, its crew shaken out like sardines from a tin. She had made him row a wide circle around the craft, tapping at each bobbing sailor with the tip of an oar like a spoon against egg before she would allow him to draw up alongside and heave a pile of freshly pleated net from the deck.

A long narrowboat, incongruous on open water, its lone blue-jerseyed captain flung halfway out over the port side, stove-in scalp like the hump of a fist punched through plasterboard. She had leant out from her side of the boat and pressed two fingers on his neck, very near the wet whitish mess of the wound, waited long minutes for any sign of life before she set about dragging the jersey over his head.

She had hung the jersey out over the bow to air for several days and had finally exchanged it for the one she was wearing with a sigh of luxury, despite its crispy sundried texture and the long bloodstain that rimmed its neck like extra stitching. Its previous owner had been a large man and it was a relief to pull it down thickly over her stomach, to hug herself around the middle and feel a heavy weave of protection over the life growing inside. She hasn't counted her months well, has no way of knowing how many more jerseys she might need to steal. On land, it would have been enough to notice a sudden change in mood, the taste of iron on her tongue, but out here on the water she is uncertain of her body, had only realised what was happening when there was nothing to be done but wait until the end.

From his corner of the boat, he does what he seems capable of doing; parcels her off the larger half of whatever food they come across, rows always in the direction of more equable weather. For the large part, he ignores the issue, inasmuch as he says almost nothing on any subject. He shivers in his undershirts when she borrows his jumpers and doesn't seem particularly bothered one way or the other.

He is better at night, softer. She thinks of it that way: with the dark, tenderness. He moves carefully into her end of the boat, rests his weight against her. They will talk, sometimes, as though they were at home, invent new episodes of television programmes they used to watch together. He misses cigarettes and bread and butter, she misses the smell of shampoo. He will describe it for her over and over – *vanilla and chemical cleanser and coconut* – and she will kiss him hard, though his face is swollen and his lips are splitting at the sides. They are both lunatic on salt water. They sleep distractedly with the weight of her belly between them.

+

Before, he had lived on a street that passed beneath a railway bridge and the gnash of the late-night overground was the soundtrack to their early time together. He had lived the way bartenders live, on an unsprung futon amid a junkyard of coffee cups, and she had spent her first weeks with him in a state of constant agony from sleeping on such an uncomfortable bed. *Fall in love with someone who makes you ache*, her mother had always told her. *When I fell in love with your father my appendix exploded. I think it was the stress.*

They had spent their time together watching movies and fucking and arguing about the movies they watched, which had turned out to be a thin but workable foundation on which to hang the best part of five years. She had loved him in a hot and cold way that relied on his eyes and his lazy way of doing things, the kindish planes of his wide-boned face.

The last October before the rain, he drove them down to the Jurassic Coast and they stayed for three days in a bungalow he had rented from his uncle. The previous week, she had had what her colleagues delicately described as a 'turn' at work – blank fall, bloody horror in her underwear – and he had skipped his evening shift to stay with her. The blood had been viscous and livid in the toilet bowl and she had cramped terribly – an ache just like her mother had claimed accompanies love. His mother was a midwife and had asked him loudly on the phone whether she had drunk a lot of alcohol or taken too many baths, done something foolish or intentional to cause this catastrophic wringing out. *You tell me she knew she was pregnant, that you both knew. You have to appreciate what that makes me think.* He had scrabbled to mute the speakerphone and later had suggested the trip as a way to distract them both.

She loved the bungalow for its proximity to the water, for its salt-frosted windows and the way it groaned and whickered like bones. During the days, she went on long walks along the beach and tried to isolate a clear emotion for the accidental thing which had bled out of her as if aware of how unwanted it had been. He left her there to swim in the water in his uncle's wetsuit and when he emerged she wrapped him in a picnic blanket because it was all they had thought to bring. She found herself trying to apologise to him without wanting to, mulish sentences that started with *I'm sorry I wasn't ready* and tapered off before *but you don't seem to mind.* At night she took his hands and devoured them, kissed the tip of each finger and tried each knuckle with her teeth.

+

The night is mauve, deep lavender. Storm colours. They circle on the water, searching hopelessly for the best direction to avoid the rain. It is a Wednesday to end all Wednesdays – frantic winds against a thrashing tide. She is exhausted and fractious and terrified of the coming downpour, slaps at his hands when he fumbles an oar stroke. *Keep going, we have to stay clear of the storm.* He glares at her in a way he will apologise for later. *Don't give me orders. I'm tired of listening to you talk.*

On nights like this, she finds she thinks of her mother at Christmas, reading to her from *Under Milk Wood*: the wide waters and moonless night, *starless and bible-black*, the deep dark falls and despairs and seas of people's dreams. She has mentioned this to him before but he is Scottish where she is Welsh and he has never read it, and she doesn't remember enough of it to recite. She wonders sometimes whether the text still exists anywhere, whether any of the sailors on any of the crafts they never approach might have been circumspect enough to grab a copy when the rains came or whether the collected works of Dylan Thomas are now universally drowned.

By little more than chance, they come at last upon a raked white outcrop which, on closer inspection, turns out to be the tip of an otherwise submerged lighthouse. It is some min-uscule hour of the night. He leans forward over his oars and his voice, when at last he speaks, is fanged with nerves. *A lighthouse means this was a shoreline, once. Maybe that means the storm won't come in this far.* She looks at him uncertainly but he is so tired the oars are slipping out of his hands and she has to jerk forward to catch one before he sets it adrift. The boat rocks with her movement and she leans back, holding herself awkwardly. Beneath the skin of her stomach she feels sudden pressure, a movement like a curling and uncurling that seems to follow the boat's frantic tipping, stilling only as the boat stills. It occurs to her that she isn't sure how she is going to give birth, out here on the water, though she shoves this thought aside with the oar which she heaves up onto the baseboards.

Sorry, he is saying now, shaking his head over the remaining oar still held loosely in his grasp, *I'm too tired, I'm too hungry, I don't think I can go any further.* She shakes her head and makes a noise which isn't an apology, though he seems grateful for it nonetheless.

They throw a rope out to the tip of the lighthouse – a painted iron finial like a candle on a cake – and tie themselves as fast as they can. They sleep like that, circling on a short cord around the drowned tower, ignoring the groan of creatures below. Things down there, growing.

+

They cross ice floes. Struggle their way through a long sequence of Thursdays in which the horizon seems always to maintain an unchanging distance – white waters at the tipping-off point of the world. One morning, they pass a curious structure which on closer inspection reveals itself to be a kind of floating town. A tottering collection of huts are stacked like treehouses atop a wide central platform, insulated with sealskin and roped around with knotted flax and cheerfully incongruous bunting. The huts are joined together by rope ladders, as though the inhabitants of each little box might have made an easy habit of clambering up or across to a neighbour and knocking on the wall. Of course, there are no neighbours. The raft is deserted. They spend an hour looting the deck for jars of whelks and lichen and hacked-up turtle meat, though neither of them has the heart to clamber up to the huts and start foraging there.

Afterwards, they brave their little boat's tilting to sit together in the stern, compiling a list of the things they miss. There is a curious tinge of competition to it, a friendly tennis match for which both nonetheless keep silent score.

I miss chocolate. I miss my hairdryer. Roast chicken. Newspapers. Paper money. Audiobooks. Fresh fruit. The sound of post arriving. Morning runs. Eating slowly. Cafetières. Frozen peas. The thought of going on holiday. Electric lights. Dogs. Wrapping paper. The way you used to look.

His face is a terrible thing to her now, weather-ravaged and unpleasant. It is as though a layer of him has come loose and is flaking away to reveal a tightness of salt; a sanding down of some hard central structure. She misses his old face – a grief she hadn't expected. *He's handsome, in his way,* her mother had told her, after they had first been introduced – coffee just the three of them one afternoon in May. He had excused himself to go to the bathroom and her mother had launched into a whispered skittle of impressions: *I like his hair, I like his accent, I think he favours his left hand.* Her mother's approval had made her feel proud of him, like some precious item she had been clever enough to spot in a sale. When he had come back from the bathroom she had folded herself into his side and grasped his wrist while her mother asked if either of them wanted to split a slice of cake. He had smiled wanly at them both, bleary off a three a.m. shift. *I'm sure he's even better on top form,* her mother had whispered in parting, souring the afternoon a little with guileless implication.

Sitting beside him in the stern, she feels the now-familiar swimming sensation in her belly and resists grabbing at his hand to ask if he feels it too. There is a sudden shriek of an oystercatcher, monstrously outsized, and he shifts backwards to watch it pass overhead. *We should get moving,* he says, and she knows he is growing increasingly anxious of the scale of things, above and below. Sometimes they see lights below the water, the bioluminescence of anglerfish and vampire squid grown too large and too close to the surface.

It occurs to her that all of them, birds and fish and sailors, have been out on the water too long. Her feet are growing webbed, although they don't talk about that. Sometimes at night he takes his apple knife to the delicate membranes between her toes, but they don't talk about that either.

+

When she was a child, she had inherited a ratty canvas tent which her mother had allowed her to drag down from the attic and sit inside. The thrill of a pretended journey had been enough to entertain her for days at a time, zipped up with her books and a beakerful of cranberry juice, imagining strange shadows dancing on the fabric walls. *You liked it because you liked four walls around you,* her mother told her later, *you liked to have things where you could see them – your little books and toys and pencils – to zip them up with you and keep them close.* It was a point made without malice and accompanied by a shape drawn in the air with fingers – an encompassing square or circle intended to illustrate a room, a tent, a boat.

She had done this once in his flat. Years later, arranging blankets and pillows into a kind of fort. She had waited inside for him to find her, coming home late smelling of pretzels and cherry brandy, peeling open the flap of her makeshift tent with one hand. *What's this, then?* He had clambered in beside her and she had put her hands in his collar, thumbed at his jaw, told him they were camping in the wilderness, the Arctic tundra, somewhere wide and flat where the sun only set once a month. *Travel, change, interest, excitement,* she had said into the dip of his neck, *pack a bag. Wherever the wind takes us.* They had been back from the Jurassic Coast only two days at this point. On the afternoon of their return, his mother the midwife had called to ask how she was doing, whether she was still cramping or spotting. *She's fine,* he had said – his voice like bad weather in another country, profoundly distant and unconnected to her – *I told you, it's better this way.*

On the bed, in their makeshift tent, they had made love in an unhurried way – his fingers, her wishbone legs. She had felt a tenderness at her hips, somewhere deep and sore, a pulling and releasing as if on some internal bell rope, and afterwards she had rolled away from him and kicked savagely at the hanging blanket until the whole structure came down on their heads. It had started to rain that night, sea rain that crusted the bricks of his apartment building like a gritting of lye, and they had slept thrown away from each other on opposite sides of the bed.

+

The whirlpool is a great, grinding Charybdis – teeth in the ocean and no clear way around it. The current is wild, dragging them in with an insistence that is something like pleading, and she screams at him to pull the boat around. He does so with the near inhuman strength of panic, wrenching them backwards with a heave of oars. She tries to help him, uses her hands – their new and delicate webbing forming paddles in the water. She watches as a bobbing school of silver mackerel is whisked past them, churning down towards the vortex.

They have to row a solid mile before they feel free of it and when they finally stop, his hands are cut to pieces by the handles of the oars. They sit panting together, bow and stern, trying to regulate their breathing against the slack easing of the current. The sky is the pink of fingertips, a tender colour. It had been a Sunday until they drifted into danger.

She looks at him and sees him lean down to wipe his shredded hands on the baseboards. His hands leave marks, twin smears which, to her, create the illusion that some sea thing has scrabbled its bloody way across the bottom of the boat before either heaving itself back overboard or being stopped in its tracks. She is overwhelmed with tiredness. She feels heavy and stretched all over, worries increasingly that whatever is growing inside her may be slowing or running out of space. She refuses to look at the bare skin beneath her clothes, isn't sure what she might see pressing up against the surface of her stomach.

From the floor of the boat, he looks up and squints at her, as though seeing something quite contrary to what he had expected. She meets his gaze, wants to say that where there is a Charybdis, there ought also to be a Scylla, but it seems an unwise thing to invoke.

+

When it happens, it doubles her up on the baseboards, a thrashing of legs and flexing hands like the beginnings of a curse. It is early morning, bruised about the eyes. She had never read baby books at home, had barely paid attention in biology, yet her body seems to follow some strange internal rhythm that feels numbered and learned by rote. The pain is overwhelming, a vast *oom*ing, waves over her head. Lurching forward from the stern to grab at her, he sets the boat rocking with a frantic jolt that makes her grit her teeth and beat him back. *What do I do*, he asks her, trying to hold her hand but finding it webbed and intractable.

The pain thickens and floods, a clenching like knuckles interlocked with knuckles, and she finds herself screaming and trying to bite her lip all at once. Black wetness, a taste like copper on her tongue. The boat careens and she finds herself thinking with a sudden sort of lunatic panic that they haven't yet labelled the day. It is too early still, too quiet to tell whether the morning will stretch its legs into a Monday or a Wednesday. The pain hits her in a fresh tide and she buckles down off her elbows, clawing fingers into the base-boards and into the skin of her own knees. A heave, a dark weight and the urge to push back against it. She clamps her tongue between her teeth until her mouth floods.

When it finally comes, it comes out writhing and not right. Too long and too thin and something less like legs and more like tentacles. It has eyes, ears, a face that recognisably echoes hers from certain angles, but its skin is not skin and its movements are the increasingly frantic thrashings of something drowning in air. A sound like a night on the ocean seeps, liquid, from the sides of its mouth. She is too dazed to react, still wreathed in pain. She finds she can only stare at the thing now careering wildly, struggling itself in useless spirals around the bottom of the boat. It is mottled all over, its movements so like the swimming motions she has become used to feeling inside her that she registers a twinge of recognition. As it shifts onto its back, she notices its spine, the dark ridge of red along the centre of its body, and she remembers the shape that had bled out of her once before – the almost-form of the thing she had not wanted inside her and hadn't known how to safeguard or to mourn.

It is only at a noise from the stern, a grunt followed by the scraping of some heavy object being lifted, that she manages to raise her head. As if from a great distance, she sees the way he is standing and what he is about to do to the thing between them. She opens her mouth to protest and finds her tongue too deeply bitten to cooperate. He has clubbed things before – large fish and great grey moray eels which he has heaved aboard with his hands and hammered at with the flat of an oar until they ceased their struggling. She knows the way his body moves before he does it, drawing in like a wire spring twisted up to full contraction before he raises his arms to beat something down.

+

When they had first fallen in love, she had kissed him with an intensity which imagined him already halfway out of the door. A grasping period – nights spent holding him overlong and too tightly, the ravenous dig of fingers into skin. Over time, this sense of frenzy had eased as she had gradually grown more confident in his staying power. It had still been easier to sleep with one hand at his wrist, but the depth of her panic had subsided a little. Most mornings, it had been possible to wake up without immediately reaching for him across the centre of the bed.

They had been together four years when she had realised she was pregnant; something she realised very quickly, almost within days of it happening. She had known her body better back then, attuned enough on land to its rhythms and weathers to notice when something was out of synch. In telling him, she had grasped at his arms and apologised and he had said very little, only releasing himself from her grip with an absent wriggle and asking, it seemed a long time later, what it was she wanted to do. That night, she had slept in strange hot fits on his futon and woken in the red-eye of the morning to find herself alone, realising after several bleary moments that he had left the room and closed the door behind him. She had lain where she was a long time that morning, tracing idle lines across her stomach and ribs and listening to him moving about in separate parts of the flat – boiling the kettle twice and leaving it, testing the smoke alarm, talking dully on the phone.

Ultimately, of course, she had only been pregnant a grand total of three months and seven days, that first time around. Even so, the memory of that morning had persisted well beyond the bleeding. A very slender sort of betrayal, the deliberate absence from a room.

+

They float. A stretch of unlabelled days. The base of the boat grows tacky with blood and very quickly begins to smell. A predatory wheeling of birds.

Without the energy to return to the bow, she remains where she is, presses her webbed hands flat against the sides of the boat as though holding herself in place. The silence swells like something bloated and threatening to spill. He sits in the stern, holding loosely on to the oar he so recently used as both club and shovel, to beat down and to heave overboard. The violence seems to have left him as swiftly as it rose, though the smell of his damp hair is an acrid reminder. Sweat. Relief and irritation. A strange reminder of nights when he'd come home from the bar wet through and complaining of rowdy patrons. Glass in between his fingers from breaking up fights.

Her mind wanders. She murmurs snatches of *Under Milk Wood*, finding she remembers more easily now as though a block has somehow loosened in her mind. She thinks of her mother at Christmas. The smell of pear cider and cinnamon, the rattle of objects wrapped in tissue paper and placed beneath trees.

Listen. It is night moving in the streets, the processional salt slow musical wind

The boat groans, heaves over the back of some vast passing creature. They hold tight and braced to capsize, but the boat only tilts for a moment before coming down again, unscathed.

+

They have seen all kinds of creatures since they first set out, one washed-out morning when they woke to find it no longer possible to cling to the land. They have passed over the heads of sea monsters, fleets of twisting cuttlefish, sea bream and Humboldt squid, dead cod and dead oarfish, miles of knotted eel floating on the ceiling of the sea. They have seen colossal things, antediluvian, too close to breaking the surface. Great Loch Ness fins and tails. They have witnessed the way things have stretched and mutated. *There are things down there, growing.* She had briefly been one of those things herself, although now she is once again her old size and shape, dwarfed in the endless increase of the sea.

The eyes are something they have never seen before. Perhaps the last thing – lambent pupils on the water. It is a night crested grey and navy and the creature which rises before them moves in a way she immediately recognises. The swimming motion she had felt in her insides and later witnessed in the bottom of the boat. It is the same but different, unimaginably larger. Tentacles the colour and consistency of candlewax. Elongated, sheen-skinned body and a face which seems to bear some unsettling resemblance to her own. If she squints, she can make out the place at the crown of its head where the oar was brought down, the battered point from which he scooped it up and tossed it overboard, bare minutes after it was born.

The night is cold, iced about its edges. In the stern, she hears him scrabbling himself upwards yet finds she cannot look away from the thing now reaching towards her. She feels a pull in her insides, that same pull she felt long ago – the tug on some internal bell rope. Somewhere low in her hips, an ache is spreading, though it is only the ghost of a pain, a shade of something already passed. She remembers it was a Tuesday on land when her first child bled out of her, though by the time the second came on the water, she was no longer very certain of time. *I'm glad you came back,* she wants to say, *whatever day it is.*

She can hear him somewhere near her, saying her name and scrabbling again for his oar, though she chooses to ignore him. Only shakes her head a little as she reaches away from him, leaning out over the side. The creature's skin, where she touches it, is warmer than expected, its reaction slower, calm beneath her hand. The boat rocks, keeling closer to the surface of the water with every passing swell. The sky is gory with stars, like the insides of a gutted night.

Acknowledgements

Writing a book is an exceptionally bizarre thing that requires a lot of exceptionally bizarre people to act like it's OK whenever you bring it up. To say I'm lucky in the people I'm surrounded by is like saying I'm lucky to have possession of both my hands – it would be impossible to do most of the things I take for granted without them, but specifically impossible to type or pick up a pen.

To the following people, I owe my entire ability to do anything:

My editor, Kish Widyaratna, for understanding everything on the kind of kindred level that, as a writer, you dream of. For patience and humour, for her fantastic company, and for leaving links to videos of glacier-calving in the margin notes, ensuring that what was work never felt like work.

Likewise, Caroline Bleeke at Flatiron (who one day I hope to actually meet in the flesh), for exceptional positivity, energy and input.

My agent, Sam Copeland, for the kind of sorely needed enthusiasm which simply isn't in my DNA. For sending an email which changed everything and for blending enormous support and professionalism with an ability to talk about *Lord of the Rings* with the depth and gravity I require. I'm unendingly grateful.

The Editors at the *White Review*, for kickstarting an incredible summer and for making the whole process with 'The Great Awake' so seamless and enjoyable.

The Curtis Brown Creative group of 2011 – not the first, but certainly the most glamorous – and Anna Davis and Chris Wakling in particular, for seeing past my then twenty-one-year-old inability to construct a sentence that was anything under a page in length.

Various people who have stemmed the descent into frothing insanity simply by existing:

Nina and Sam Harvey-Brewin; Sarah Crowden; Lucy Quintin-Archard (Baraona) and the QAs at large; Emma Waring, Gabriella Shimeld-Fenn and Hannah Leach (hexagonally and with great love); Sophie Jagger, birthday twin preferable even to Sandra Bullock; Daisy Johnson, for kindness and enthusiasm in the face of a thousand other commitments; Lindsay Smith and Kerry Richmond, whose collective nickname I won't put down in print; Eleanor Harris, Who I Met In A Queue And Accompanied Around The World; Cordelia Masters and Ed Harper, Jess and Ash Burton, Amanda Williams and Pete Quigley (hey GANG); Alex Wilson and Emily Down, fake brother and fake sister extraordinaire.

Izi Woodger, with whom ten years' friendship has passed

ACKNOWLEDGEMENTS

in ten minutes, despite the weathering of several peculiar house shares. For her humour and insight, for her time.

Rosalie Bower, for turning up at the right time and staying. For being able to read (contrary to popular opinion), for patience and love, for midnight chicken, for shark movies, for all that.

Sarvat Hasin, without whom nothing here would exist. For being the best, most talented and most utterly necessary of friends. I could make a list of the stories in this collection which wouldn't have been written without her, except I already have, and it's the whole collection.

My brother Nick, for doing me a solid and embarking on at least as economically precarious a career as writing, presumably to take the heat off me. Having a brother who is also a best friend is a particularly brilliant thing, and I'm grateful for *The Simpsons*, for *Round the Horne*, for *The Santa Clause* and for anything else with which we have ever successfully alienated people.

Lastly my parents, Polly and Laurie, who read to me before I could read and acted as though writing wasn't a wholly ridiculous thing to want to go and do. I love them entirely and this book is for them, even the gross bits.